P9-APD-516

Immigrant City

Also by David Bezmozgis

The Betrayers
The Free World
Natasha and Other Stories

Praise for *Immigrant City*

"[Bezmozgis] shows that his skills at creating perfect (and perfectly unsettling) worlds-within-worlds remain unparalleled."

—NANCY WIGSTON, *Toronto Star*

"David Bezmozgis's latest book of short stories focuses heavily on moral complexity and immigrant experiences, highlighting the author's uncanny ability to write sensitive, sympathetic prose." —*The Globe and Mail*

"David Bezmozgis deepens his exploration of the fates and furies that beset Jewish immigrants as they struggle with the unwieldy claims of the past. Replete with the wry humour and finely hewn prose that characterized the author's debut, *Natasha and Other Stories*, this new collection resonates with power and poignancy." —*Quill & Quire*

"Bezmozgis' way with this material is at once funny and sad. This happy stylistic mixture runs through the stories in *Immigrant City*."

—*The Canadian Jewish News*

"Cultures in collision; no one does new Canadians and their lives better than Bezmozgis." —*Toronto Star*, Top Ten Books of the Year

Praise for *Natasha and Other Stories*

"Bezmozgis's pointed, emotionally resonant tales are so elegant they seem destined, like [Isaac] Babel's, for anthologies of classic fiction."

—*The Globe and Mail*

"Remarkable short stories. David Bezmogis [has] a gift for swift, sharp storytelling."
—*National Post*

"A generous, witty account of boyhood . . . rich [with] reverberating pathos [and] a sensualist's delight in language. . . . Impressive."

—*The New York Times Book Review*

"What sets [Bezmozgis] apart . . . is his quiet command of unadorned language, his wry humour and his keen understanding of the human heart."

—*Winnipeg Free Press*

"Scary good. . . . Not a line or note in the book rings false." —*Esquire*

Praise for *The Free World*

"A delicious drama of ambivalence and excitement. . . . The vigour of the book's characters is achieved in the remarkable way Bezmozgis puts words together."
—*Maclean's*

"Bezmozgis makes good on the promise of his celebrated first book, *Natasha and Other Stories* (2004), in his spectacular first novel. Sharply funny and fast-paced, yet splendidly saturated with intriguing psychological nuance and caustic social commentary."
—*Booklist* (starred review)

"Bezmozgis displays an evenhanded verisimilitude in dealing with a wide variety of cold war attitudes. . . . An assured, complex social novel whose relevance will be obvious to any reader genuinely curious about recent history, the limits of love, and the unexpected burdens that attend the arrival of freedom."
—*Publishers Weekly*

"Impressive. . . . Bezmozgis is a remarkably polished and proficient writer whose sentences are neatly trimmed and sharply focused. . . . Bezmozgis is unquestionably one of the star writers of his generation. He not only grapples with an important modern story, he does so with undeniable authenticity and intelligence."
—*Quill & Quire*

"Bezmozgis proves why he was recently proclaimed one of *The New Yorker*'s 20 Under 40; this is mellifluous, utterly captivating writing, and you'll live with the Krasnansky family as if it were your own."
—*Library Journal* (starred review)

Praise for *The Betrayers*

"David Bezmozgis has a dazzling talent, is the possessor of that rarest of skills—the ability to create fiction which is intensely serious but which also vividly encompasses the absurdity of life."
—Scotiabank Giller Prize Jury

"Extraordinary."
—Barbara Gowdy

"*The Betrayers* is an endlessly fascinating exchange of philosophical views and a character study of great depth and nuance, made all the more effective because of its compact structure and swift pace of narrative."
—*National Post*

"Powerful, thought-provoking [and] deftly plotted."
—*Maclean's*

Immigrant City

Stories

DAVID BEZMOZGIS

HARPER **PERENNIAL**

Immigrant City
Copyright © 2019 by David Bezmozgis
All rights reserved.

Published by Harper Perennial, an imprint of HarperCollins Publishers Ltd

First published by HarperCollins Publishers Ltd in a hardcover edition: 2019
This Harper Perennial trade paperback edition: 2020

Some stories in this collection were previously published in a slightly different
form: "Immigrant City," *Tablet* magazine; "How It Used to Be," *Zoetrope: All-Story*;
"Childhood," *The Walrus*; "Little Rooster," *Zoetrope: All-Story*;
"Roman's Song" (published as "The Proposition"), *Harper's Magazine*;
"A New Gravestone for an Old Grave," *Zoetrope: All-Story*;
and "The Russian Riviera," *The New Yorker*. Special thanks to the editors
of the earlier versions of these works.

No part of this book may be used or reproduced in any manner whatsoever
without the prior written permission of the publisher,
except in the case of brief quotations embodied in reviews.

HarperCollins books may be purchased for educational, business,
or sales promotional use through our Special Markets Department.

HarperCollins Publishers Ltd
Bay Adelaide Centre, East Tower
22 Adelaide Street West, 41st Floor
Toronto, Ontario, Canada
M5H 4E3

www.harpercollins.ca

Library and Archives Canada Cataloguing in Publication information
Title: Immigrant city : stories / David Bezmozgis.
Other titles: Short stories. Selections
Names: Bezmozgis, David, 1973- author.
Description: Second edition. | Previously published: Toronto, Ontario, Canada:
HarperCollins Publishers Ltd, 2019.
Identifiers: Canadiana 20200159011 | ISBN 9781443457811 (softcover)
Classification: LCC PS8603.E95 A6 2020 | DDC C813/.6—dc23

Printed and bound in the United States of America

LSC/H 9 8 7 6 5 4 3 2 1

To Iris Tupholme

Contents

Immigrant City / 1

How It Used to Be / 17

Little Rooster / 39

Childhood / 75

Roman's Song / 91

A New Gravestone for an Old Grave / 113

The Russian Riviera / 167

Immigrant City

I HAVE THREE DAUGHTERS. One is a baby. One is seven and prefers to stay at home. One is four and wants to come with me wherever I go, even to the drugstore and the bank. If I don't take her, she cries.

Recently, backing out of a tight parking spot, I damaged the front passenger-side door of our car. I heard the sound of metal against concrete, the sound of self-recrimination, dolour and incalculable expense.

In the aftermath I called my wife, who was born in America and raised in mindless California abundance. For her family, scratching cars and misplacing wallets was like a hobby. I, on the other hand, had been an immigrant child, with all the heartache and superiority that conferred. We ate spotted fruit. I told my wife what I had done; her response was less than sympathetic.

I called the car dealership; I called a local body shop; I called a number tacked to a telephone pole. Then I called my uncle Alex, whose greatest fears were identity theft and getting a bad deal. He told me of a Serbian mechanic who, if you paid in cash and didn't ask any questions . . . I started dialing the Serb's number when I remembered the year was 2015 and the incompatibility of my uncle's fears. On a classifieds website I keyed in the make and model of my car door. Who knew? Didn't every kind of flotsam wash up on the blasted shores of the Internet, including a black 2012 Toyota Highlander front passenger-side door? Indeed, there one was, offered for sale by Mohamed Abdi Mohamed of Rexdale. In the accompanying photo, taken on an apartment balcony, the sun glinting off its immaculate finish, it looked just like my door before I'd mangled it. I sent Mohamed a text. He texted me back. I counter-texted. Soon we had a deal, consummated in texts.

There are a number of practical questions that could be posed at this point. Presume my wife posed and I answered them. However, there are many different considerations in life, and *practical* is a relative term. Perhaps buying a car door from a stranger on the Internet isn't the most practical decision, but I was viewing the thing in existential terms. I was asking: Who am I? How far have I strayed from my formative self? What—*ai, ai, ai*—is the song of my soul?

The next morning, I prepared to go get my door. My wife needed the car for work, but that didn't deter me.

"How do you plan to get it home?" she asked.

"Like an immigrant."

As I put on my shoes, Nora, my four-year-old, sidled up to me. "Where are you going, Papa?"

"To get the door."

We were in that aimless interval between the end of summer camp and the start of the school year. A nanny was looking after the baby, and the two older girls were either fighting or intertwined in front of the television, a lazy fan spinning overhead.

"I want to come with you," she said.

"It's far," I said.

In anticipation of my answer, she made ready to cry.

I reflected: Wasn't this precisely the sort of trip my daughters needed? What did they know of the real world? While they ate take-out sushi, Syrian refugees were being tear-gassed by Hungarian cops, and Greek grandmothers, flayed by austerity, were walking off rooftops.

My oldest daughter resisted all coercion, so Nora and I set out on the journey by ourselves—first by streetcar through our gentrifying neighbourhood, then by subway to the end of the line, almost to the airport. By the last stop the train had nearly emptied out, leaving few representatives of white privilege. Those who remained looked pallid and desiccated, as if they'd been too weak to flee with the others.

At the station we boarded the number 45 bus that would take us up to Dixon Road. Nora is a particularly pretty child;

old women are forever touching her face. On this bus too, where most everyone might have been a relation of Mohamed Abdi Mohamed's. Nora didn't mind. She is very companionable. A bearded man beside us was reading a book, which she misheard as being about the five pillows of Islam.

From the bus stop, it was not far to Mohamed Abdi Mohamed's address. On either side of the street rose apartment buildings, thrumming with life and larceny. There it was, my immigrant childhood.

"Papa, are you crying?" Nora asked.

"When Papa was a little boy," I began.

We crossed a green lawn. We saw a modest playground. A little girl in a hijab was swinging very high. We saw a basketball court without any hoops. We saw a mound of trash composed of broken furniture and discarded strollers.

On benches in front of the building, Somali women in traditional dress turned their eyes to us. Four security guards stood by the entrance doors, wearing grey uniforms and body armour. We were in what was known as a "priority neighbourhood."

In a long list of Mohameds, I found my Mohamed. A friendly, gravelly voice bade us up. The door buzzed. Worn carpeting, dim lighting, elevator walls scored with initials.

"Smell," I said to Nora. The acrid spice of life wafted from every door.

Mohamed was in the hall waiting for us. Somalis are commonly tall and thin. Mohamed was tall and thin. He had a handsome, sculpted face, and a high, regal forehead.

"Very nice," he said. "I also have a daughter."

In addition to the daughter, he had a son and a wife, who greeted us wearing a long dress and a lavender hijab. The daughter, the same age as Nora, wore shorts, a T-shirt and a sparkly pink hijab. The boy was eating his lunch, a chicken drumstick clutched in his little fist.

I confided to Mohamed that I too had been an immigrant boy. That my father had garbled the English language, and that my mother had cooked chicken drumsticks, which I had eaten, often cold. Mohamed nodded. Fraternal understanding passed between us.

"Would you like to see the door?" Mohamed asked.

"Yes," I said.

"It is upstairs," Mohamed said, "at my uncle's apartment."

I looked over at Nora. She had joined Mohamed's daughter in combing the mane of a plastic horse.

Mohamed intuited my concern.

"Your girl can stay here. She will be happy. My wife will watch. Upstairs is just men."

The mind descends quickly to dank depths. Mohamed had never mentioned an uncle before. I thought: If I am dismembered upstairs, what will happen to Nora? Or what if upstairs is merely a ruse? Mohamed's wife and children seemed harmless and kind, and I hadn't forewarned Mohamed that I was bringing my daughter, but what did I know of Somali folkways? When I was a baby in Soviet Latvia, a Gypsy woman had once walked off with my unattended stroller. My father too had nearly been taken by Gypsies. Such things happened. Humans trafficked other humans for vile ends. It didn't seem wise to bring Nora upstairs, and it didn't seem wise to leave her behind. The wise decision was to take my child and go home, but I didn't want to offend Mohamed. What if I were mistaken? Not seconds before, he and I had shared in a moment of genuine spiritual communion. What stock could be placed in feelings if we were so quick to disregard them? And would I have been so quick to disregard them if Mohamed hadn't been Muslim and black? Then again, what price enlightenment? Surely not a father's love for his young daughter. Before we'd left the house, Nora had asked me to put her hair in a ponytail and I had done it. If you have done it, then you know that this is an experience of the most tender and terrifying love, for which you would readily give your life.

"Nora, I need to go upstairs for a minute," I said. "Is that okay?"

Nora was in a pony and unicorn phase, so I had to repeat myself before she looked up and mouthed, "Okay."

Mohamed guided me out the door and into the mouldering hallway. As I followed him, I reflected unhappily upon my character. It occurred to me that my problem was not indecisiveness but inconsistency. It wasn't that I was incapable of being firm, only that I couldn't reliably predict when I would do it. This was somehow worse.

We rode the elevator up six floors, the mechanism churning, Mohamed smiling benignly. As we ascended, marijuana fumes filtered into the chamber. When the doors opened, my first breath was coarse-edged. From one side of the corridor came the sound of young men's voices. I turned to look, though Mohamed deliberately did not. Three Somali teenagers peered back at me with proprietary insolent swagger. One lifted his T-shirt, as if to expose a gun in his waistband—only there was no gun. His friends laughed and one called to me, "You looking to score, motherfucker?"

Mohamed seized me by the arm and pulled me after him. "Those are not good boys," he said. "Even if in school you are only a black face and the manager of the doughnut shop will not give you a job, it doesn't mean you should become like this."

We ended up at an apartment at the opposite end of the corridor from the boys. Mohamed knocked three times in quick succession, paused, and knocked twice more. After a time, a young Somali man with a sleeping bag draped about his shoulders opened the door.

"*Assalam Alaikum*, brother," the man said.

"*Alaikum Assalam*," Mohamed replied.

The man stepped aside. In the entryway there were at least a half-dozen pairs of shoes, mostly sandals, neatly arranged. Mohamed added his pair to their number, and I did the same. Before us was a room almost entirely devoid of furniture. Several overlapping rugs covered the floor. Along the walls, men appeared to be sleeping, their faces concealed under blankets or sleeping bags to shield them from the bright daylight. None of the men stirred when we entered, and even the man who'd admitted us returned to his place on the floor and drew his sleeping bag around him. There was one young man, also Somali, who wasn't sleeping. He sat on the floor, his back to the balcony, typing rapidly on his laptop. He wore large headphones and glanced up only briefly to register my and Mohamed's arrival. The only other person in the room was an old man seated in a brown leather armchair. He was dressed in a white shirt and black trousers, his feet bare on the rug. His face was smoothly shaven, and under a white woven skullcap, his grey hair was carefully trimmed. From where I stood in the doorway, his face was presented in profile. It took a moment for me to apprehend that he was blind, his visible eye milky and unseeing.

"Hello, Uncle," Mohamed said, and bent to kiss him on either cheek. Mohamed motioned for me to draw near.

"This is the writer," Mohamed said, though I'd never told him my occupation. For a moment I was unsettled by this, but I was also aware that my reaction was dishonest. In the age of the Internet, I was frankly surprised and disappointed whenever I met someone who hadn't troubled himself to acquire the basic and easily accessible information.

Mohamed bade me kneel down by his uncle's chair. The old man faced me and put his hands atop mine, as though to divine or communicate something through his smooth, dry palms.

"In Somalia, before the civil war," Mohamed said, "he was minister of justice. But warlords captured him. Tortured him. Took his sight."

I thought the old man would say something, but he didn't speak. Perhaps the warlords had also taken his speech. He continued to regard me with his sightless eyes and to gently cradle my hands in his. This lasted for what seemed like a long time, though neither he nor Mohamed behaved as though it were in any way peculiar.

Eventually Mohamed said, "Come."

He went to the door that opened to the balcony. He pulled it open and stood in the aperture waiting for me. As I approached, Mohamed turned to the young man with the laptop and issued an order in Somali. The young man shot Mohamed a harsh, resentful look but nevertheless removed his headphones and rose to his feet. He left the room and disappeared down the short hallway that led to what I imagined was the bedroom.

On the balcony the car door was concealed under a white tablecloth. Mohamed lifted the tablecloth and exposed a door that looked exactly as advertised. While I inspected it, the young man whom Mohamed had sent on his errand stepped out onto the balcony and handed Mohamed a warped sheaf of pages bound with rubber bands. There followed a terse exchange in Somali between Mohamed and the young man, which concluded with the young man clicking his tongue at me disparagingly and returning inside.

"Pay no attention. It is just Abdirashid," Mohamed said. "He is clever and loyal but he is distrustful of Jews."

"Mohamed," I said, "I have to ask: Who are these men, where did you get this door, what is happening here?"

"My uncle is dying," Mohamed said. "These men are here to care for him. For Somalis, he is a national hero, the people revere him, he could have been very useful to America and Canada, offered his counsel to kings and presidents, but nobody cared to ask. They neglected and forgot him like he was trash."

At this point Mohamed extended the sheaf of papers to me.

"These are his memoirs. It is a great story. A million people should read it. There is war, love, family, power, land, God, magic. It needs only a writer. I took your book from the library. At the story of the old Jew dying, I wept. I thought, That Jew is my uncle."

Mohamed pressed the pages on me.

"Mohamed, I don't know anything about Somalis," I said.

"Nobody knows. That is the problem," Mohamed said. "If you just read the papers, the car door is free."

"Is that your only copy?"

"No, Abdirashid has a file on his computer."

I agreed to take the papers, but only on the condition that Mohamed understand that I would probably never write a single word about his uncle.

"If you read the pages," Mohamed said, "I am confident you will write this story."

People were always offering writers their stories, I thought. But those were rarely the stories writers wanted. Those stories were like children who always raised their hands in class. Good stories didn't raise their hands.

I paid Mohamed the sum we had agreed upon, and he helped me carry the door into the apartment. We stopped so he could fetch a satchel for the manuscript. I stood beside his uncle with the door resting against my hip. The old man, seated as before, started to hum an ancient dirgelike tune. It resonated deep in his throat, like a prisoner in a cave.

Mohamed returned with the satchel, and I slipped my arm through the loop. We carried the door together out of the apartment. It was heavier than I'd expected, but I thought of the Syrians, the Iraqis, the Afghans, the Eritreans, the Sudanese, as well as my father, my grandfather and all my persecuted forebears.

In the corridor the same boys were still getting high. Again, Mohamed did not deign to look at them. I tried to follow his example. Still, we knew that we were the objects of their laughter and scorn.

"Yo, Mohamed," one boy called. "How's the caliphate?"

Mohamed spun and barked something in Somali, but it made no impression. They continued to laugh as Mohamed glared at them with steely tight-lipped ire. Our elevator arrived; the heavy metal doors enacted their grim choreography. Mohamed faced the panel and brooded upon the blue illuminated numbers, while I was conscious, as I sometimes am in elevators, of winching down a narrow shaft on dusty cables in the dark.

From the elevator we trod wordlessly to Mohamed's apartment. When he opened the door, I saw Nora sitting rigidly on the sofa, her face puffy and tear-stained. Mohamed's wife fussed about her, pinning a pale blue hijab around her face. Once she spotted me, Nora's eyes darkened with hurt and anger. Fresh tears formed and ran down her cheeks.

"You left me alone," she said.

"I'm sorry I scared you," I said.

I opened my arms, and quick to shed her anger, Nora ran over and hugged my legs. I placed my hand atop her hijab and felt the warmth of her little head emanating through the soft fabric.

"She was very sad," Mohamed's wife said. "So we made for her this gift."

I noticed Mohamed looking on approvingly, his old amiability returning, as though he'd received an antidote to the toxins from upstairs. The entire family accompanied us to the elevator, Mohamed helping once again with the door. When we parted it was with the proclamations of bosom friends or relations, not strangers who had engaged in a bizarre commercial transaction.

Alone in the elevator, Nora and I regarded each other. "Papa," she said.

"Yes, my love," I replied.

"When can Samiya come over for a play date?"

"I don't know," I said.

Nora studied me for a moment and elected not to press the matter. "Is it true you met a big teacher upstairs?" she asked.

"I met somebody," I said.

"Samiya's mom said you were meeting a big teacher."

"I met a sick old man."

"Oh," she said.

I reached over to stroke her head. As I started to loosen her hijab, Nora recoiled. "You know you don't have to wear that anymore," I said.

"But it's mine," she said in the injured tone she used whenever I tried to take anything away from her.

The elevator arrived at the lobby. I thought of how one might explain to a four-year-old the raft of complicated, legitimate and paranoid reasons that militated against her wearing her gift in public, but the mere prospect of opening my mouth felt hideous and exhausting. I was also aware that I was a man with a car door who feared that Nora's hijab would make us weirdly conspicuous.

In the end it didn't matter. In an immigrant city, a city of innumerable struggles and ambitions, a white man with a car door and a daughter wearing a blue hijab attract less attention than you might expect. People, after all, are immersed in their devices and concerns. On a crowded bus or a packed subway car, they do not necessarily surrender their seats. It wasn't until the streetcar that we finally got two seats together.

Nora had the window, the breeze blowing in; I had the aisle, the door propped up so that I too was looking through a window. The streetcar rocked Nora to sleep in my lap. When our stop approached, I nudged her gently. Her hijab had slipped down over her brow. Drowsily, she opened her eyes.

"Nora, it's our stop," I said. "Do you want to go home or keep going?"

"Go home and keep going," she said.

How It Used to Be

FOR THE SIN OF the cross look. For the sin of the terse reply. For the sin of the damp towel on the floor. For the sin of the intemperate purchase. For the sin of the selfish minute. For the sin of undermining my fucking authority with the children. For the sin of repeating yourself for the thousandth time. For the sin of the frigid silence. For the sin of never accepting responsibility. For the sin of not seeing yourself. For the sin of not apologizing and for the sin of apologizing too late. For the sin of treating you like a stranger. For the sin of not showing affection. For the sin of not appreciating me even a little bit. For all these, not to mention others, we stood in the doorway, with my Uber parked outside, its hazards blinking, and the neurotic fever dream of my plane crash reverberating between us in series with my lurid carnal opportunism should the plane not go down.

From upstairs the littlest one called for "Mama." The middle one ran to the door, hugged my legs and said she was going to miss me so much. The oldest one was somewhere in the house, squatting on the floor, turning the pages of a graphic novel. Something crashed to the ceiling above our heads. The littlest one called more insistently for "Ma-ma."

"I have to go," my wife said. "Enjoy your trip."

For the sin of deliberately misconstruing my trip.

Reza M, my Uber driver, younger than me, waited by the trunk of his cobalt blue Honda Civic. We engaged in a courteous pantomime over my carry-on, then I took my place in the back seat and looked at my house. It had stood there for ninety years. How many families had filled it with their swirling involvements? I only knew the people we'd bought it from, of whom no instrument could now detect any trace.

The car moved and my house slid away. Two strollers casually deposited on the porch and a silver scooter flat on the ground. Some rocks the children had collected, painted and named. Beside the garbage and recycling, a red plastic car with a seat and a steering wheel and an orange hood that accumulated rainwater. Yellow dandelions in a lawn that needed cutting. And in the flower beds, our drooping peonies, their frilled heads grazing the dirt.

I thought, My God, what if it's really the end this time? Misery and euphoria seized my heart and for a moment I felt like I might be sick. To calm myself I addressed the back of Reza's head. His dark hair, freshly barbered, was like a solid block between the pink vulnerability of his ears. And his posture was that of a schoolboy from a land where posture was still respected. With so many clues it wasn't hard to guess the land, but Reza was nevertheless impressed that I had done it. I impressed him further by reciting a few assorted facts about his country. He corrected me on the last.

"It was wrong of the CIA and the British to meddle in our affairs," Reza said. "But my countrymen who mourn Mossadegh are very naive. Name me one country that is not Norway where the oil is nationalized and there is democracy. Mossadegh has been made into a martyr, but if he had succeeded he would have been a thief. Other things are also known about him, but they are improper to talk about."

Reza then asked for my relevant details. The country of my birth: a place that technically no longer existed and that I'd left before I was old enough to put on the red neckerchief of the Young Pioneers. My profession: a thing I rarely confessed to because of some relation to the sacred, the profane and to doubt—also because the word *writer* made people feel guilty and confused and caused them to say things they didn't mean.

The purpose of my journey: a conference about which I could say little more than that I'd received an invitation from someone I didn't know representing an organization I'd never heard of. Such things occasionally happened. Because I was always worried about money, every time I checked my email it was with the faint, pathetic wishfulness that it would happen again. This time it was to join a group of "thought leaders" for something called FICNIC, The First Immersive Continuum Narrative Innovation Conference. Travel, accommodation and a $2,500 honorarium were provided—the honorarium applicable in full against a possible engagement contract. I also needed to sign a non-disclosure agreement.

"Technology," Reza reflected. In his home country he had studied computers. Now he was back in school pursuing accreditation while also doing IT for a local Persian media company and driving Uber. His wife was at home with their two children and would soon give birth to a third. Every day he thanked God.

We had arrived at the airport.

"What's your secret?" I asked.

"There is no secret. We are no different from the birds and the fishes."

We exchanged a congenial farewell and I went inside the terminal to catch my flight to Montreal. Less than two hours later, I was met at the gate by a man who held a sign with my name on it. He was a short, pot-bellied black man, his hair and beard salted with grey. He wore tan slacks and a tan windbreaker with the emblem for Continuum Visions—the V contained within the C—stitched over his left breast. As I approached he brought his cellphone to his mouth and said, "*J'ai le dernier.*" He gestured for me to follow him and apologized for his English—"Haiti."

We exited the terminal and walked along a line of hotel and car rental shuttles until we reached one painted the same colour as the man's clothes and with the same emblem inscribed on its side. The doors were open and the Haitian man slid into the driver's seat. I was greeted by a pretty young woman with a calm, authoritative manner. Behind her were several rows of seats, two each on either side of the aisle. Nearly all the seats were occupied by cerebral, insular and distracted men and women who made no conversation but gazed ahead, read documents or scanned their devices. Pinned to each person's breast was a round white badge with a bold black upper case *B*. One was also affixed to the young woman's blouse. She told me I would find mine in my welcome package. We were Group B. It was a condition of our participation that we wear our badges.

The shuttle brought us to a hotel in downtown Montreal, not far from the university campus where I had once been a student. When I'd accepted the invitation, it had also been to return to a place where I'd once been very happy so that I might breathe the mist of residual happiness that still adhered to the buildings and the streets. As we descended from the highway into the city, I perceived myself as I had been, eager for romantic adventure, sometimes bold. Rue du Fort: a girl from another university, whose name I could no longer remember but whom I could see outlined against her bedroom window, anachronistically wearing a slip, a white shoulder set against dark hair. Afterwards, like a hero in an art film, I had walked home in the rain, the only person on Sherbrooke Street as far as the Ritz.

In my hotel room I leafed through the welcome package. Included with the badge was a glossy brochure about Continuum Visions written in vague, grandiose language. There was a photo and bio of Continuum Visions's founder, a square-jawed, shaven-headed man who'd made his fortune by starting and selling a company that facilitated something revolutionary and intrusive with email. Later, he compounded his fortune by starting and selling a second company that undermined the first. The names of the companies, those of their illustrious buyers, and the routinely mind-boggling purchase prices were all listed. The package also held a concise conference itinerary, the location of Continuum's offices, detailed instructions about transport, and staff contact information.

I sent a text to decline the transport and walked as if following several paces behind my younger self. He descended the steps of the walk-ups in which he'd lived from year to year. He read a book by the window of a small diner run by a family of Greeks. In the bars and restaurants along St. Laurent Boulevard—and the ghosts of those bars and restaurants—he faltered or triumphed in rounds of impassioned talk. Across from Parc du Portugal, he deposited a fan letter in Leonard Cohen's mailbox. He desperately wanted to become. The yearning was so intense it assumed shape and mass, like a stone in his hand or upon his chest. At first it was a solitary yearning, then a joint one—the life we would make together—before it was solitary again.

St. Laurent to St. Joseph Boulevard. St. Joseph to Clark Street. Half a block north and I stood in front of the house where I'd spent hundreds of nights. I could have found it blindfolded. I tried to conjure what it had all felt like. It came back in random fragments:

Outside, it's dark. I'm on the black futon couch in my apartment, watching television. I lift the phone from its cradle. Lauren says, "I'm done with my paper. Come over."

In the brief warm spell at the beginning of the school year. We are on her stoop. She brushes a strand of hair from her face and teaches me how to roll a cigarette.

"Elbows on your knees, knees together, close your left eye and hold your breath."

"Really?"

"No."

The morning after I first slept in her bed. Her roommate is packing her lunch at the kitchen counter. Frost gleams in the windows. I hang by my fingertips from the moulding above the kitchen door like a contented animal and then pull myself up.

We sit reading side by side in bed. She wears her high school volleyball jersey, an artifact from another life. Without looking up from the page, I slide a hand under her shirt and cup her breast. It is cool and smooth against my palm.

It happened, I thought. Years after you left here and ceased to know her, the lofty thing you dreamed of came true. You made it come true. What a comfort it would have been to know that. And what a surprise to learn that in twenty years you'd be standing here looking back with a longing equal to the longing with which you'd once looked ahead.

The Continuum offices were in Mile End, where tech companies had set up shop in a neighbourhood of students, artists and Hasidic Jews. Fairmount Avenue. A famous bagel shop. St. Viateur Street. Another famous bagel shop and the red brick edifice of St. Michael's church, with its green-domed campanile. Across the way, Café Olimpico, proclaiming stubborn authenticity.

I kept on and saw a white limestone building, a converted corner bank branch. From a distance it looked like it had been appropriated by a film shoot. Two heavy black curtains, the width of the sidewalk, hung down to the ground from poles that extended from the roof. They subdivided the building into three sections: along one street, at the apex and along the perpendicular street. A motorcycle cop diverted pedestrians to the opposite sidewalk. As I came closer, a shuttle like the one that brought me from the airport stopped at one side of the building. A young woman with a clipboard descended and watched as the other passengers exited the shuttle and entered the building through a set of double doors. I pinned my badge onto my blazer and crossed the street. In the instant she noticed me, I realized that, though she wore the same outfit and was of similar colouring, height and build as the woman who met me at the airport, she was a different woman. Her badge had an upper case C.

"You're not supposed to be here," she said sharply. She

drew the curtain away from the wall and peered behind it. She faced me, let the curtain fall and instructed me to follow.

We skirted the sidewalk, passed through one curtain and saw nobody. The "B" woman from the airport waited beyond the second curtain, looking displeased. The "C" woman regarded her with open scorn. She said nothing to the "B" woman and vanished after delivering me into her care.

"Transport was not optional," the "B" woman said. "The others are already inside."

She led me briskly into the building. The curtains extended inside as well. To our right, one went from floor to ceiling, from the entrance doors to the open doors of an auditorium and beyond. To our left, a broad glass and steel staircase configured up to the second storey. Visible through it were parallel rows of smoked glass cubes—offices.

We proceeded into the auditorium, which was the size of a small-town movie theatre. A floor of exposed concrete sloped gently down to a circular stage of pale wood, which was where the curtain ended. Blended, unintelligible speech sounded from behind it. The woman indicated for me to find a seat among my group. There were quite a few empty seats. Clipped to the back of each one was a curved, mirrored face shield, as for a cosmic welder.

I took the nearest seat, beside an imperious, dark-haired woman in a black sleeveless top and jeans. She wore heavy silver bracelets and a large hammered gold ring. Lines of text in an alphabet I didn't recognize were tattooed on her inner forearms.

She raised an eyebrow in allusion to the general oddity.

"Performance art or sociological study?"

"Or a diversion for a rich man."

"Yet here we are."

"So it seems."

"And what offence did you commit?"

"Probably something I wrote."

"Let me guess, you're a grovelist?"

"Grovel, grovel. And you?"

"A poet and playwright. Mainly of the Armenian diaspora."

The lights dimmed with their hushing effect and a real or simulated female voice welcomed us to the conference and invited us to put on our visors. I freed mine from the back of the seat and found it nearly weightless, like a promise of the future. I brought it down over my brow, causing something within it to awaken and form an impalpable band around my head such that it hovered there by mysterious means. Two white rubbery crocus tips emerged, which I inserted into my ears and felt intuitively expand to fill the cavities. The sensation was comforting, not disturbing. Our youngest daughter had lately developed a tic of putting her index fingers in her ears before she performed an action. Fingers in ears; cover the doll with the dishtowel. Fingers in ears; add another blueberry to the line on the plate. Without ever trying it ourselves, we feared what it would portend if she didn't outgrow it. We'd become adult, quick to condemn harmless pleasures.

Through my visor I looked at the Armenian poet and playwright, who now seemed crisper, better articulated, as when the correct lens is snapped into place at the optometrist's. Reflected in her visor, I saw my own otherworldly head, and hers reflected, Escher-like, in mine. She turned away to look around the room, and a kind of eruption coalesced around me in the form of a crowd on a barren hill. A scorching sun beat down upon us. Men dressed in caftans and rags shouted, wailed and surged toward a cordon of implacable Roman legionaries. An emaciated cripple lay on a wooden pallet by my feet. A group of lepers, their faces gnawed by disease, moaned deliriously and offered their hands to the sky. I recoiled as a filthy bandage brushed my cheek, but nobody noticed me. I felt like an onlooker at the spectacle, present but immaterial, while still myself, with my critical mind, wearing the visor, in the auditorium, in Montreal. I gazed up and saw the three crucified men, the middle one in the crown of thorns and with the sign above his head, *Iesus Nazarenus, Rex Iudaeorum*. The nails had been driven into his palms and his crossed feet. Blood streamed from those wounds and the places on his body where he had been scourged. I saw his face framed by the lank hair, the eyes blue and terribly lucid, the features somehow familiar. Bearded men of higher rank, their garments trimmed in indigo, shouted in the Talmudic language I had learned poorly as a boy and mostly forgotten. But it didn't matter since an English translation was superimposed in the sky.

"You who would destroy the temple and rebuild it in three days, save yourself."

"If you are the Son of God, come down from the cross."

A crucified man beside Jesus derided. "You trusted in God, let him deliver you now, if he will have you."

Jesus looked to the heavens and cried out. "My God, my God, why have you forsaken me?"

A navigation interface appeared above my left shoulder. It read:

Matthew

Mark

Luke

John

And then switched to:

Matthew

Mark

Luke

John

The scene before me was halted and reset. Once again, the lepers moaned and offered their hands to the sky. The filthy bandage brushed my cheek. The Sadducees and the Pharisees railed.

The criminal beside Jesus spoke. "If you are Christ, save yourself and us."

"Where is your humility?" demanded the second criminal. "Do you not fear God? We are getting our just rewards, but this man has done nothing wrong." He appealed to Jesus.

"Remember me, Lord, when you come into your kingdom."

"Today you shall be with me in paradise," Jesus said.

Supernatural clouds gathered and blotted out the sun.

In a strong, clear voice, Christ called out. "Father, into your hands I commend my spirit."

The breath of life left him and his head fell to his chest.

The scene froze and another index appeared listing the Christian denominations. In quick succession, I saw before me the Christ of Byzantine iconography; Russian; Ethiopian. Anatolia, Rus and Kush cast their mark upon his flesh. Under "Catholics," subcategories rendered the scene in the high reverent style of Michelangelo, the sober precision of van Eyck, the tragic malevolence of Caravaggio and the golden derangement of Lippi.

A heading for "Jews" and Christ disappeared entirely, leaving only two crosses on the hill.

A heading for "Atheists" and I was on a street in ancient Galilee, looking through the window of a modest house. Inside, Jesus planed a cedar board. Shavings dropped to the ground where a small boy handled intricately carved animals—a horse, a lion, a hare. A young, pregnant woman entered the room, carrying a meal of bread, olives, cheese and wine. She glanced down at the child, who sprinkled shavings onto his toys and conducted a private, polyphonous dialogue with them.

"Simon isn't disturbing you?" she asked.

"No, he's a good boy," Jesus replied.

She set the food down on a low table. Jesus watched her affectionately. He stopped his labours and lay a hand on her belly. She looked to him, smiled and kissed him on the lips.

Everything dissolved into whiteness except for Jesus, who was no longer Jesus but the shaven-headed, square-jawed man from the corporate brochure. In place of the caftan was a charcoal grey tailored suit with a white shirt, open at the collar to reveal a lean, tanned, sinewy throat. The blue eyes burned with the same prophetic conviction they'd possessed on the cross.

"The life of anything is like a journey between two shores," he said in an urbane middle-European voice, gravel rolling in a copper drum. "You depart from one shore and do not see the other. After a time, you begin to sense it. Those birds flying, where did they come from? You glimpse the outline with its dark topography. It fills you with terror. You draw nearer and apprehend its particularities. Now it starts to seem less forbidding. You realize that it is actually awesome and beautiful. When it is very near, you are impatient to arrive. 'Hurry, hurry,' you say to yourself. 'Let me be delivered unto it.'"

He paused and allowed the blue light in his eyes to cool.

"What you have just seen is the other shore. Gospels, apostles, mutability, Rashomon. We have been moving toward it for millennia, and lately ever faster. Many of you have feared and dreaded it, cursed your ill luck that it should happen in your lifetimes. But fear and dread only stifle your own progress. The transmission of ideas through the old methods is a dying man, kept alive by habit and sentimentality. Shed a tear if you like but do not leap into his grave. For ages we wrote and read because we could fashion nothing better. We imposed a monopoly on expression, perpetuated a hierarchy of truth and legislated dominant versions of history. This only endured because it was profitable. It is now the opposite, tedious. I offer you here the chance to shape a new vision of the future by contributing your version of the past. Each of you has been invited because you are an expert in a knowledge area that has been algorithmically determined to be of great popular interest. For instance, you are an authority on the Manchurian Incident. The American Civil War. The Bolshevik Revolution. Auschwitz. The Crusades. The Partition of India. The Six-Day War. The French Revolution. The Kennedy Assassination. The Moon Landing. Christopher Columbus. The Creation of the Earth. But since it is not for us to arbitrate truth, in a different group there is someone who espouses a rival vision, and possibly another and another. None is given precedence or privilege. We do not condescend. Ultimately, it is the consumer who will—"

I removed the buds from my ears and lifted the visor from my face. They released their grip without resistance and went dormant. Around me the others sat upright, their heads tracking in subtle uniformity. I walked out of the auditorium, proud of myself for taking ten virtuous steps even as I knew I probably wouldn't take twenty. It would have felt good to take a firm moral stand, to set an example for my children, but I anticipated my wife's reproach. I'd accepted the trip, left her with the girls and come back empty-handed because I wanted to be a hero. As if we could afford it. As if I wasn't the one who agonized, complained, lost sleep—but when someone finally presented me with an actual opportunity? Other people found ways to compromise. She had. What about all the things she'd given up? Performing. Travel. Her body. Another voice interrupted. It was also hers. *Oh, please. If you want to ditch it, ditch it. Don't pretend I'm stopping you. As if I'd ask you to work with cranks and Holocaust deniers.* And then tearfully, *You're so quick to think the worst of me.*

I stood in the lobby, trying to separate thoughts and feelings that had muddled together and made it impossible to decide anything or even to understand quite what I was deciding. People now passed, employees of the company, mainly young men of the type I expected to find in such a place, going this way and that, joking, making small talk, or striding with concentrated purpose, like office workers anywhere, attending to their designated tasks, contributing their minute adjustments on the world. I fell in behind a group of them. They crossed under the staircase and split off into their respective offices. I wandered on by myself, glancing absently at the doors. Instead of letters or numbers, they were identified by symbols. On one was a cyclone, on one a pine tree, still another showed a kitten, an apple, a heart. The heart door opened and a man stood facing me, almost as startled as I was but quick to recover. He was older than the other employees, more my contemporary, slightly rumpled, wearing eyeglasses, his curly hair thinning and receding. He looked at his wristwatch and grinned.

"You're with the visiting group?"

We both noted my badge.

"You're a little early for the tour."

"I was just walking around."

"Unchaperoned?" he said in mock alarm.

"I can leave."

"The others are still in the presentation?"

"Yeah."

"But you weren't sold?"

"I don't think so."

"Well, it's not for everybody."

"I guess not."

"Just most people!" he said, and laughed.

I assumed our exchange was over and retreated a step to let him pass.

"Come in," he said. "I'll give you a private tour of what we're doing in here. I think you'll like it."

He held the door for me. I'd expected the room to be large, but it was small. There were three workstations, wedged closely together. One belonged to my host; one was unoccupied; a young woman perched at the third. She wore oversized headphones and gazed at a screen that displayed hundreds of snapshots, some of which appeared to be actual photographs, others selfies from profiles and social media streams. She typed rapidly on her keyboard, causing certain of the photos to balloon hugely, undergo some cosmetic manipulation and then shrink back.

"What you saw before was the blockbuster. Here we make the indie film. Éric Rohmer, John Cassavetes. Similar tools, different objective. But the next step in art. A little closer to the time machine."

On hooks along the rear wall hung a row of mirrored visors. He reached over and plucked one up.

"There's someone in your life you want to see again, living or dead, we can materialize them. Your departed grandmother. Dad who walked out on you. The family dog. Your high school sweetheart. Or your wife, the way she was when you first met. Providing there's pictures and video available somewhere. Metadata. Archive. Cloud. We'll find it, filter it, and fuse it with your memories."

He offered me the visor. "Want to try?"

I accepted as an electric beep sounded at the door.

"Hello, Jan," greeted my host.

Wearing the charcoal suit and white shirt, bald Jesus came in. He smiled and wagged his finger at me as at a naughty child.

"*Aga, vot kuda ty podevalsya, tovarishch*," he said in slightly accented but fluent Russian. ("Ah, so that's where you disappeared to, comrade.")

"*Popalsya*," I replied. ("You caught me.")

"Has he chosen yet?" Jan asked.

"No."

"This is my favourite room," Jan said. "Isn't that true, Randy?"

Randy nodded.

"My first time, I materialized Milena Ruzickova. Twelve years old. What sweet hours we spent in the shed where the builders kept their tools. Milena, Milenka, how you broke little Janek's heart!"

Jan gripped the back of Randy's chair and wheeled it around for me. He placed his hands on my shoulders.

"You disapprove of my project. You think Jan is a revisionist, a nihilist—God forbid, a capitalist!" he said.

"Does it matter?"

"Only subjectively," he said. "But never mind." He paused a moment and asked, "Do you know whom you'd like to materialize?"

"Yes," I said.

"Good," he said. "But I'll spare you the trouble."

"How's that?"

"Uncle Jan will decide for you. Like in Communist times when nobody had a choice and everyone was happy."

The visor and the earbuds and you're in the white sweater, which we dubbed "favourite sweater," with the little roses embroidered at the collar. You wore it the day I noticed you by the parking garage and the first time we went out. It's a vintage, schoolmarmish thing, but you're twenty-two and beautiful and it adds to your charm. How long now since I saw it or even gave it a thought?

We come out of the movie theatre, searching for our car and the pigeon flails at the curb, one wing grotesquely bent, blood beaded on the pavement. It flaps crookedly, spins around on its side, rests, peers at us, spins again. More than a memory, it feels like I'm in the crystalline bowl of my old life. I see a rock, a phone book in the doorway of a tutoring centre. You take off your sweater and edge toward the curb. "I can't," you say, and hand me the sweater. The bird pecks and thrashes as I wrap it up. I feel its every sharp and brittle movement. It doesn't submit, hurting itself, even after I bundle it against my chest and then hold it in my lap as you drive, looking for a vet, convinced we have to save it, unwilling to let it die.

Little Rooster

TEN YEARS AFTER MY grandfather died, I found myself sorting through a shallow plastic bin that held the accumulated documentation of his life. My mother had labelled it in Russian: "Mother and Father." When she downsized from a house to a condominium, the bin migrated to me. It is humbling to consider that, to all extents and purposes, a human life can be contained inside a shallow plastic bin. It is even more humbling to consider that it can be contained in *less* than a shallow plastic bin. My grandfather had been a thrifty, patient and meticulous person who didn't like to throw anything away. Besides, who knew when some relevant authority might demand a full accounting? Sentiment had stayed my mother's hand but I intended to be ruthless. One old Israeli bus pass is poetic; one hundred are oppressive.

My grandfather was born in a small Latvian town during World War I. His first languages were Yiddish and Latvian. Traditional Jewish schooling and an interest in Zionism contributed functional Hebrew. He also had some Russian, which he was later obliged to cultivate as a soldier in the Red Army and over four decades as a Soviet citizen. Though he spent the last twenty years of his life in Canada, he never learned English. Of the things worth keeping in the bin were various photographs, passports, notarized English translations of birth certificates, a marriage licence, the official acknowledgement of my grandfather's front-line service during World War II, a clinical description of the wounds he sustained and the consequent benefits afforded him by the Soviet state. There were two sets of claim forms for wartime reparations—a legitimate one to the Germans for their crimes, and a spurious one to the Swiss for their laundering of "looted assets" itemized as:

Two houses, furniture, dishes, jewellery $100,000 US (approx.)
Store with leather shoes, leather furniture $300,000 US

There were also numerous letters written in Russian and in Yiddish. My Russian wasn't good enough to decipher the cursive script, but millions of Russian-speakers—including my mother—could do it. The Yiddish was another matter.

Once the vernacular, it was now the preserve of academics. I knew one, a professor at the University of Toronto, who was writing a monograph on heteronormative bias in Galician graffiti.

I made an appointment and brought the letters to her office. Some were from my grandparents' friends, resettled in Düsseldorf; others, postmarked from Israel, were from my grandfather's younger brother, Venyamin, affectionately called Venya. I knew Venya only from stories told to me by my mother and grandfather. I knew, for example, that when he was a boy, a horse had stepped on his head. He'd nearly died. For the rest of his life, he bore a dent in his skull in the shape of a hoof. After the war he married a Jewish woman, reputedly unkind. They had two children. The first was a son, the spitting image of Venya. The second was a daughter, exceptionally beautiful, who strongly resembled a Latvian who'd lodged temporarily in their house. Later, it emerged that Venya also had an illegitimate child, a blond girl, raised by her maternal grandparents.

Though unwilling herself to do the work, the professor connected me with one of her graduate students, a tattooed Norwegian named Knut, who agreed to write a summary of each letter for a standardized fee. He explained that this was a common way for Yiddish students to supplement their stipends. A generation of Jews appealed to them with their inherited glyphs. Most often the letters were banal, but

occasionally something interesting, even scandalous, surfaced. A secret in the secret language. Knut preferred when
this didn't happen. People got upset and Knut suffered
moral qualms about profiting from such disclosures. He'd
consulted the Talmud for guidance, but to no avail. The
sages diverged.

Two weeks after I turned over the letters, I met Knut
at a popular, as yet unboycotted, Israeli coffee franchise
near campus. Though he greeted me warmly, I detected
unease. He began with the innocuous Düsseldorf corre-
spondence, which concerned itself mostly with the realms
of health, education and finance. Who was hale and who
was ill. What afflictions had stricken. Who, *thank God*, had
prevailed and who, *God forbid*, had succumbed. Also, the
inexorable passage of the brilliant grandchildren through the
stations of the school system. The admirable and incom-
prehensible directions they pursued in life. The exact
dollar figures of their salaries and the purchase prices of
their homes. Venya's letters mostly conformed to the same
model. It was only in his last four letters, sent in the six-
month period between my grandmother's death and his
own, that the substance changed significantly. Faithful to
our agreement, Knut had summarized these as well, but he
cautioned me to reflect before I took possession. He didn't
pretend to understand the implications of everything he'd
read, but he believed the letters touched upon matters of a
delicate nature. It was possible, of course, that what he'd

read in the letters was already common knowledge to me and my family. And perhaps, even if it wasn't, I might not be disturbed by what he'd uncovered. People had different sensitivities. However, from the tone and context of the letters, Knut suspected that they addressed something confidential between my grandfather and his brother.

Though I was tempted, I took Knut's advice and resolved to reflect. One of life's cruellest lessons is that a person can't *unknow* something. And there exists enough unavoidable pain in the world that one would be a fool or a masochist to actively court more. My grandfather, whom I loved very much and whose essence was still sometimes palpable to me, was dead ten years. His brother, a man I didn't recall ever meeting, was dead seventeen. What did I stand to gain by scavenging through the past? The reflexive answer, of course, was that sacrament, the Truth. After all, it was just a cruel stroke of history—perpetrated by the dread mustached visages—that explained why I couldn't read the letters myself. And would my grandfather have kept them— like so many Israeli bus passes—if he didn't want them to be found? Perhaps the sin wasn't of trespass but of laziness and indifference? How many vain and useless things had I done while these letters languished, humming with meaning? And wasn't there a privileged kind of knowing available to us only after our loved ones were gone? In other words, I walked around the block and justified doing what I already wanted to do.

Summary of letter from Venyamin Singer to Berl Singer,
   6 March 1999

*Venyamin asks after Berl's well-being. He repeats his
condolences on the death (January 1999) of Berl's wife,
Shayna—a generous heart, loved by all—but reminds Berl
that the living must live. He asks if Berl has returned to
the Latvian Canadian Cultural Centre and if he has been
able to verify that the woman he saw there was Lauma.
He admonishes Berl not to let the matter drop. He concludes with affectionate wishes.*

Summary of letter from Venyamin Singer to Berl Singer,
   30 March 1999

*Venyamin praises Berl for persisting re: Lauma. He
remarks upon the mysteries of fate. He dismisses Berl's
reservations and apprehensions. (There is an uncontex-
tualized allusion to homemade farmer's cheese[?].) He
insists Berl act decisively and make contact with Lauma.
He concludes with affectionate wishes.*

Summary of letter from Venyamin Singer to Berl Singer,
   9 May 1999

*Venyamin congratulates Berl on Victory Day (Great Patri-
otic War). He reproaches Berl for the pessimistic attitude
he displayed during their telephone conversation (date
unspecified). He says he has slept poorly since the conversation, worried about Berl. He relates his attempts to*

book a flight to Toronto. He cites his course of chemotherapy and his doctor's refusal to write a letter of permission (to airline). He criticizes his doctor, the Israeli healthcare system and the airline. He insists he feels well but is not naive about his prospects. This explains his sense of urgency re: Lauma. He says she is the love of his life. He concludes with affectionate wishes.

Summary of letter from Venyamin Singer to Berl Singer,
   3 July 1999
[NB: Handwriting illegible in some places.]
Venyamin asks after Berl's well-being. He apologizes for his long silence. He experienced complications from the surgery. He blames (a commander?) for (the pills?). (Electricity?) in his hand makes it hard for him to write. He confirms that he received Berl's last letter. He says (the sisters?) stole the photograph Berl sent of Lauma. He asks that Berl send another. He encloses a photograph of himself taken in the (??) fortress. He also encloses a letter to Lauma. He asks Berl to relay it. He recalls a different letter he asked Berl to deliver to her. He hopes Berl has (??) (vagina?) (this time?). He concludes with affectionate wishes.

I didn't share with my mother what I'd learned from Knut. The subject of my grandparents' deaths remained raw for her. She still drove to the cemetery nearly every Sunday to visit their graves. If the trail of Venya's letters led somewhere unsettling, I couldn't see how that knowledge would do her any good. However, under the pretext of trying to make sense of disparate bits of my grandfather's files, I asked her if she knew the name *Lauma* or if she'd ever been to the Latvian Canadian Cultural Centre. She didn't recognize *Lauma*, but not long after my grandmother's death, she had visited the Latvian Centre with my grandfather. The Latvian government, having partially crawled out of its post-Soviet hole, announced that it would offer pensions to eligible expatriates. My grandfather qualified, and my mother took him to the Latvian Centre to help process his application. It was the only time she'd been there. Though she'd lived half her life in Latvia and now, by virtue of her age, was receiving her own modest Latvian pension, she found no reason to return. The Latvian she'd learned at school, she'd mostly forgotten. Her language was Russian. She was Jewish. And she was leery of ethnic Latvian expatriates, most of whom had retreated with the Germans at the end of the war or descended from people who had retreated with the Germans. What they had or had not done to Jews, or why they might have preferred to retreat with the Germans rather than be "liberated" by the Soviets, was too esoteric a consideration. Simply, she didn't feel comfortable with them.

Without a car, the trip from my grandfather's apartment to the Latvian Centre required three buses. It was hard for me to imagine my grandfather making such a trip on his own. I couldn't recall him venturing anywhere by himself. He seldom even went to the nearby supermarket for groceries; my mother and aunt handled the weekly purchases for him—not because he was physically incapable but because his lack of English made the task inconvenient. If he had a doctor's appointment, someone in the family drove him. The grocery store, the doctor's office, a family gathering—did my grandfather go anywhere else during the last decade of his life? His synagogue was on the ground floor of his building. Maybe he went for a stroll in the park across the street or sometimes attended a different synagogue a block or two from home, but I wasn't even sure about that. To the extent that I thought about my grandfather when I wasn't with him, I pictured him scrupulously engaged in some mundane task in the circumscribed precinct of his one-bedroom apartment. I certainly didn't imagine him embarking on an hour-long, multi-stage journey to a distant part of the city. But a spry and surprisingly attractive nonagenarian Latvian woman confirmed that he'd done it quite regularly.

She'd known him as Berls Singers, the Latvianate version of his name. I encountered her at the entrance to the dining hall, seated at a table, ticking off the names of the seniors who attended a Thursday afternoon social club. As we spoke, the members of a folk choir finished their rehearsal and descended from a stage at the front of the hall. The singers were elderly Latvian men; their piano accompanist was an elderly woman. All had approached their efforts with vigorous and joyless determination, as if at once proud and resentful at having to bear so disproportionate a cultural burden.

The woman was surprised to learn that I was Berls's grandson. In all the time he had frequented the Latvian Centre, she had thought him alone in the world. No family member had ever accompanied him or come to watch him perform with the choir. He'd been circumspect, so she hadn't pried. To live a long life was to accrue many joys but also many hurts and disappointments. She remembered my grandfather as a quiet, mild-tempered man who possessed a beautiful singing voice and a remarkable memory for Latvian poems and songs.

As she spoke I sensed her subtly inspecting me. She asked my name, and to ingratiate myself I offered the Latvianate version, which sounded foreign coming from my mouth. She inquired if I spoke Latvian and I conceded that I did not. She asked where I was born and was enthused to learn it was Riga. She, too, had been born there. A half-century before me. She'd last seen it in 1944, when she'd fled with her parents. I volunteered that I'd left with my parents in 1979. I'd imagined that from my grandfather's name and physiognomy, she would have deduced he was a Jew, but her reaction led me to wonder. Maybe she'd known and forgotten? In any event, the little yellow pilot light did not come on. We smiled at each other as we each performed the sordid calculations. Innumerable faces, voices and landscapes swirled in the silence between us. Boxcars rolled to the east and west.

A commissar and an SS officer shouted orders in a hoarse voice. A crow landed on a corpse.

Despite whatever the woman had deduced about my origins, she invited me to stay for lunch. The centre's kitchen prepared traditional Latvian foods and offered them at a reasonable price, and was particularly renowned for the baked goods. If I was curious about the centre, I could sit and talk to the other diners. They would be happy for the company. I observed them at their tables—most chewing silently or conversing in muted tones—and tried to imagine my grandfather among them. The men of the choir were rigid, silver-haired, peasant-faced. They wore suit jackets and narrow ties after a Latvian folk pattern. When I'd seen my grandfather surrounded by his contemporaries, wearing an ordinary tie, it was for the complimentary kiddush after the service at his building's synagogue. He'd be one of a dozen or so elderly Soviet Jews loading paper plates with herring, honey cake and egg salad, and allowing the more boisterous of the group to pour down-market whiskey into his Styrofoam cup. In a room loud with joking and grumbling, my grandfather was usually reserved. I'd always taken it as a function of individual temperament rather than a manifestation of national character. But it was dawning on me that I'd underestimated and under-imagined him.

With one question answered, I posed the other.

"We have more than one Lauma," the woman said, "but I think I know who you mean."

"My grandfather would have known her."

"Lauma Gulbis. In her day she walked on air. It was very sad how she ended. The more God gives in your youth, the more He takes in old age. Her daughter is Agnes. She lives in her house."

....

There was a courtyard in the Latvian Centre with green patio tables. I took a seat to place my call to Agnes. Around me, paralegals drank coffee and smoked cigarettes during a break in a seminar. There weren't enough Latvians to cover the overhead, so the community let space and offered catering. I could tell that the paralegals were only negligibly aware of their surroundings, as if to convey that life, already taxing, would be untenable if one took heed of every abstruse thing dear to strangers.

They paid no attention to me, either, sitting by myself, daunted at the prospect of making a phone call. The initial momentum that had propelled me forward had stalled. It had been easy to come this far. Contacting my professor friend at U of T and Knut the Norwegian had seemed like a game. Dropping in on the Latvian Centre, like an adventure. But calling a woman out of the blue to pose intimate questions about her dead mother seemed like only an unwelcome intrusion. Then again, had I not passed the point of no return when thought became deed? And wasn't the world already strewn with too many half-consummated acts? I didn't want to contribute another.

I dialed the number I'd been given—a number, I was told, that had been in operation for fifty years—and heard a woman answer. I ascertained that she was Agnes and then tried, as succinctly as possible, to explain who I was. There was a drawn-out silence on her end when I asked if she knew Berl Singer, as though she wasn't so much trying to place the name as decide whether or not to avow what she knew.

"Is he still alive?" she asked.

"No, he died ten years ago."

"Well, I'm sorry to hear that," she said, and fell again into a tempered silence.

I filled the silence by telling her that I'd recently discovered a reference to her mother in my grandfather's documents and was curious to learn about her and the relationship she'd had with him, since he had, for some reason, kept it a secret from his family. I'd hoped to determine why.

"I can't answer that question for you," Agnes said. "He never spoke of any family, so I had no reason to believe he was concealing anything."

"What did he speak of?"

"The past. My mother was already not well when he encountered her. Alzheimer's. He reminisced with her about people they knew in their youth."

"I'd like to hear more about that," I said.

"You want me to recite conversations from fifteen years ago?"

"I'm sorry if it sounds strange."

Agnes fell silent once more, although this silence felt gentle, ruminative.

"You couldn't know, but you have called on my mother's name day. So maybe it isn't purely accidental. I'm now in my kitchen baking a cake in honour of the day and will celebrate it with my daughter, who is practically the only person left with whom I can reminisce about my mother."

....

Agnes's house turned out to be not very far from my own, twenty minutes by bicycle. I rode there in the late afternoon as we'd agreed, a bouquet of red carnations jouncing in the basket before me. The neighbourhood had once been Polish and Hungarian but was gentrifying like every other in the city. Young professionals with children and enigmatic resources were eradicating the old houses and replacing them, often as not, with narrow modernist boxes, architectural lexicon for "Fuck off, old." Any of the remaining original homes looked like poor relations, stubbornly or haplessly impeding progress. Agnes's was one of these, flanked alternately by a cube and a construction site. As I rode up I saw a blond woman smoking a cigarette in the shared lane between Agnes's house and the cube. She eyed me sullenly as I came to a stop, dropped her cigarette on the pavement, ground it out with her boot and disappeared through a side door. Her terse revulsion evoked the usual countervailing response. I presumed this was Agnes's daughter and imagined, against reason and practically against my own will, the illicit possibilities. The heart barks like a dog.

I walked my bicycle up the driveway, past a Japanese compact car, to the steps that led to the covered porch, which was painted a pale blue. To the right of the front door, set against the brickwork of the house, two patio chairs with striped blue cushions faced the street. To the left, a large ceramic pot blazed with pink geraniums. Before I reached the landing, Agnes was waiting at the threshold, regarding me in a flat, unsmiling, almost clinical way. She appeared to be in her sixties and altogether reconciled to the fact. She wore no makeup, and her grey hair was gathered in a simple ponytail level with her shoulders. She had on a cream-coloured sleeveless blouse and roomy denim shorts that fell just below her knees. On her feet were brown orthopaedic sandals. The only adornment she'd permitted herself was a silver necklace with an amber pendant and earrings to match, like an affirmation of Baltic heritage. My mother owned similar things.

Agnes directed me to lock my bicycle to the balusters. As I knelt to secure the device, she watched me silently. When I'd finished with the awkward business, she remarked on my resemblance to my grandfather. Now that I'd crossed into my forties, I'd noted the same thing about myself. Though, peculiarly, the resemblance wasn't just to him, but to all my male relatives in their more advanced years. It was as if some primordial, Jewish oy-face had surfaced with time, rounding and softening features, imbuing a fatherly, grandfatherly, even ancestral lachrymosity as from the headwaters of the biblical patriarchs.

"I look nothing like my mother," Agnes said. "The resemblance skipped a generation. Ruta, my daughter, inherited my mother's looks, but not much else."

I removed the bouquet from my basket and followed her into the house. We walked through a dim foyer—to the left, a staircase led to the upper floor; to the right, an archway accessed the living room. Another archway separated the living room from the dining room. In other words, the rooms were small and dark, closed off from one another.

Agnes ushered me into the kitchen, where a glass door offered a view of the backyard. It was late September, and the leaves of the Norway maples cast a copper wash over everything. On the table Agnes had set out a kettle, teacups, plates, forks and three-quarters of a cake.

"The cake I baked for my mother's name day," she said. "We're only two women; we could never finish it."

She took the bouquet of carnations from my hand and motioned for me to sit at the table while she went to the sink. I watched her deftly free the flowers from the plastic wrapping, separate out the blooms, count them and then snap one of the stems in half and deposit it in the trash.

"I'm sorry," I said. "I thought the superstition against even-numbered flowers was only Russian."

"Who knows who borrowed from whom," Agnes said.

She trimmed the remaining stems, filled a vase from the tap and set them in water.

Framed on the kitchen walls were several small amateur watercolours of regional songbirds and a larger charcoal drawing of a cat. There were also photographs: a posed portrait of an elderly couple—presumably Agnes's parents—taken on the occasion of some notable life event, and a more recent snapshot of a young woman in bulky workwear—a reflective vest, green hard hat and protective goggles—standing inside a monumental garage, dwarfed by the treads of a gigantic front-end loader. Though her features were obscured by the hard hat and goggles, it was obviously the woman I'd seen smoking outside.

Agnes brought the vase to the table, cut each of us a slice of cake and commenced to pour tea. She noted my interest in the drawings and photographs.

"My mother painted the birds and drew the cat. The birds she did from pictures in books. The cat she did from memory. It was her cat, Mitzi, from Latvia. When she and my father fled the Russians, she brought the cat with her. All the way to Germany. Imagine that. For three years Mitzi lived with them in the DP camp, but she didn't make it to Canada."

"Very lifelike," I said.

"My mother was very talented, very artistic. My father was also talented, especially with his hands. He kept a wood shop in the garage where he created beautiful things. Figures. Sculptures. Also traditional Latvian musical instruments. Maybe in another life they could have been recognized for their gifts. But for people of their generation, from simple families, from small provincial towns, they had limited opportunities. My father finished the eighth grade; my mother the sixth. It's amazing they accomplished all they did."

"I felt the same about my grandparents," I said.

"Come," Agnes said, rising. "I'll show you something."

I followed her into the living room, where, hanging by braided leather straps along a wall, in the shape of a V, were three trapezoidal, dulcimer-like instruments. Agnes took one down and presented it to me. It was made of pale wood—pine or birch—and was decoratively carved in the Latvian style, the minimalist suggestion of a sun for the resonant chamber, and runic designs that resembled intersecting swastikas above the tuning pegs.

"You can hold it," she said.

It felt quite solid, heavier than I'd expected it to be. "What is it?" I asked.

"A *kokle*," she replied, disapproving of my ignorance. "You play it by resting it on a table or on your lap. That is the Latgalian *kokle*. There is a Kurzeme *kokle*, but it is smaller and has fewer strings. My parents were from Latgalia, same as your grandfather, and so my father preferred the Latgalian *kokle*. He made many of them. A few, like these, he kept. The rest he donated to the community. Not just in Toronto, but across Canada and even the United States. Chicago, for instance. Also Texas."

"Did he play them?"

"He made them; my mother played them," Agnes said, looking wistfully at the instrument in my hands. "She played also when your grandfather visited. When she wasn't capable of doing much else, she could still play. She played and he sang. I think it was a great comfort to her. Perhaps to him, too."

I tried to imagine my grandfather in this room with the elderly Lauma—she with the *kokle* on her lap, he sitting next to her singing Latvian songs. I supposed it was a touching scene, but so much about what Agnes described didn't add up. How extensive was the secret life he'd led? Not only was he making furtive trips by bus to the Latvian Centre in one end of the city, but also travelling to Agnes's house in another. He never had a cellphone, and my mother, aunt and uncle called him routinely. If he didn't answer, nodes of panic would aggregate like birds on a roof and occasionally erupt in a spasm of flapping.

I asked Agnes, "What did you know about my grandfather?"

"Not very much. He told me he was a friend from Balti-nava, from my mother's youth. After my father died, I used to take my mother to the Latvian Centre. Her mind was going and she was depressed and confused by my father's death. At the Latvian Centre, people knew her. They looked after her. I could leave her and run errands. One afternoon I came back and found her sitting at a table holding hands with a strange man. Your grandfather. Then he started coming to the house."

"By himself? He didn't speak English."

"I gave him directions in Latvian."

"Had your mother ever mentioned him before?"

"No, but she wasn't one to talk much about her past."

"When the two of them spoke about the past, what did they speak of?"

"Do you know what it's like to care for someone with Alzheimer's? If you can get a moment to yourself, you take it. He came here and they talked or sang. It gave me a chance to cook, to clean, to wash my hair. I didn't sit over them and listen to every word."

"I understand. But did you possibly hear them talk about his brother, Venyamin? Venya?"

"Not that I recall."

"My grandfather never delivered a letter from him?"

"A letter to my mother?" Agnes regarded me as if I were impaired. "In her condition, what would she do with a letter?"

I understood that my line of inquiry would lead nowhere. Either my grandfather had been a master of concealment, careful to divulge nothing to Agnes—as he had divulged nothing to us—or Agnes had been, and continued to be, a party to the subterfuge. Why that might be, I couldn't comprehend. I felt myself gripping the *kokle* very tightly. That I still held it compounded my sense of frustration and foolishness. I relaxed my grip and set the instrument on the sofa.

"Agnes," I said, "can I ask you one more, possibly very stupid, question?"

"Ask whatever you like."

The question was gratuitous and indulgent, but I persisted anyway.

"I didn't know that he was or was not a Jew," she replied.

When we parted at the front door, Agnes regretted if I was disappointed with my visit and that she'd been unable to provide me with the information I'd sought. She had tried, in advance of my arrival, to locate a video she'd shot of her mother and my grandfather together—her mother playing the *kokle* and my grandfather singing. But she'd been unable to find it. She pledged to try again and to call me once she did. I could return and we'd watch the video together.

....

It was dusk when I rode home to my wife and daughters. Under the darkening canopy of trees, I flowed along residential streets as though indistinguishable from my thoughts.

What had I learned from Agnes? My grandfather had visited Lauma at her home. They'd sung parochial songs and talked about things Agnes could not recount. When it was no longer advisable, he'd stopped coming. That was the sum of what Agnes had given me. And after Agnes, the trail went cold. There was nobody else who could shed light on what had motivated my grandfather to keep visiting Lauma in her reduced state. She was a sick woman. It wasn't as if they were engaged in some love affair. And even if they had been, what would have been the harm? She was a widow; he was a widower. Why choose to withhold it from us? Unless his intention was to withhold for the sake of withholding. To have something altogether his own. A secret like a muscle built up for his own delectation, which nobody else could see but which he could flex and feel. A sense of firmness in the core, when everything else was deteriorating. A small claim to autonomy or wildness in the face of neutralizing domesticity. Or was I ascribing my own impulses to him? In life, I'd never thought him capable of reasoning this way. But what did I know about the limits of his mind? Apparently, not enough. And apparently, that was how it would remain. I would have to resign myself to it.

At home I was drawn into the eddies of our evening ritual. There were grievances to adjudicate and half-hearted punishments to mete out. There was bargaining and cajoling over math homework and piano practice, interspersed with earnest and playful affections. There was fitful conversation, dinner, dishes, toilet and bedtime. All the while, looking at the faces of my wife and children, I felt the attenuated weight of my grandfather's secret. It was a small fraction of what he must have felt. He'd kept a secret while I was keeping the secret of a secret—and one I understood only partially and imperfectly. Maybe because of that—because there really wasn't anything definitive to say—I didn't tell my wife where I'd been or what I'd been doing. Or it may have been out of a sense of fealty to my grandfather, as though, as his only male grandchild, I had an obligation to keep faith with him in death as I'd kept faith with him in life. When nobody else could summon the patience, I'd listened to exhaustive recollections about his beloved pre-war Baltinava. And his repeated accounts of being wounded at the front and his long and arduous recuperation. Were someone to ask me, I could name the surgeon who saved my grandfather's arm. Posterity would know him as Dr. Dubinsky.

To regain our psychological equilibrium after the rigours of bedtime, my wife and I repaired to our individual screens, she in our bedroom, I downstairs in my office. After ingesting my dose of the day's cultural and political news, I checked my email and found a message from Ruta Gulbis. Its subject line read: "Your grandfather."

Hi David,
You were just at my mom's house. I'm sending you the video. I don't know what she told you, but it probably wasn't the truth.
Ruta Gulbis
780-404-8001

I clicked on the file and encountered Lauma sitting on the sofa in Agnes's living room. She wore a grey skirt and pale-yellow sweater. In her lap she cradled a *kokle*. Her expression was vaguely fearful, as if she expected to be scolded for some indeterminate offence. A woman's voice sounded off-screen, presumably Agnes's, saying something in Latvian. Lauma didn't so much as twitch. A moment later my grandfather walked stiffly into the frame and sat near Lauma. He wore burgundy house slippers, dark trousers and a striped shirt with a blue tie under a blue-and-red argyle vest he'd favoured. As Lauma watched him take his seat, her expression changed from anxious to impassive. My grandfather glanced at her, as if to ascertain her mind, and turned calmly to face the camera. Agnes spoke again and he nodded. The camera then zoomed in on his face, immediately zoomed out, adjusted focus and jerkily panned over and down to reframe him and Lauma so they were centred on the screen. All the while, my grandfather appeared and behaved exactly like himself, patient and obedient. I felt a powerful rush of feeling surge up in me, which manifested itself, surprisingly, in Yiddish. My mind formed the phrase: *Berl, vos tostu?* It translated, not harshly but endearingly, as "Berl, what are you doing?" It was an echo of the way my relatives—my father, my uncle— would greet my grandfather in his apartment or at one of our houses. Before switching to Russian, they'd offer one or another phrase in Yiddish, delivered mostly in jest, like an acknowledgement of their legacy membership in a quaint but defunct club. Meanwhile, in the video, Lauma's fingers started moving across the strings of the instrument. She played a short introductory passage, and then my grandfather launched into the lyrics with his strong, confident voice. It was a happy, jaunty tune—odd in the context. Even though I was ignorant of most things Latvian, I recognized it. It told of a little rooster impatient to wake the sleepy village girls.

I'd heard my grandfather sing it before, in the guise of Latvia's national folk song. I watched him and Lauma perform it to completion, whereupon Lauma removed her hands from the *kokle* and Agnes applauded. Agnes then uttered what sounded like a request for another song, but Lauma rose from the sofa. My grandfather also began to rise when the video abruptly ended.

I sat quietly for a minute, the black screen before me, and considered exactly how I would proceed. It was nearly ten o'clock. Ruta had written not a full hour earlier.

Modern technology furnished too many alternatives and confused what should have been a simple matter. I wanted to speak to Ruta. But when did I want to inform her that I wanted to speak to her? And then when did I actually want to speak to her? And what was appropriate based on the timing and the content of her email? Each succeeding question didn't so much bring me closer to an answer as cause me to despise myself and the culture I lived in. In the end I composed the following text: "Hi Ruta. It's David. Thank you for the video."

Immediately, I saw the ellipsis blink in the respondent's bubble.

I told my wife I was going for a walk and sat on a bench in the park near our house. During the day the park teemed with nannies and children. Plastic playground equipment had been installed atop a spongy surface, and a set of swings fixed over a sandpit. Beyond the playground were an open field, a knoll, a mix of young and mature trees where dogs ran and relieved themselves, sternly warned to keep clear of the children. At night, these same dogs streaked unrestrained across the entire park while their owners chatted. Sometimes teenagers got high and behaved obnoxiously on the swings. During warmer months, shadowy characters hunched at the edge of the park, and in the mornings parents and dog owners found spent condoms and hypodermic needles. As I waited for Ruta, I had the park mostly to myself. Occasionally someone walked or cycled past. In a far corner, dog tags tinkled around the glow of a cellphone.

From the bench I could see cars turn from the main road onto our street. I inferred which was Ruta's—a silver Dodge Ram pickup with Alberta plates that slowed several houses before ours and crept forward. I went to meet her where she parked. Through the window, she appeared younger than I'd originally thought, closer to thirty than forty. She met my eyes briefly, then leaned across the passenger seat to retrieve something. As Agnes had conceded, Ruta was beautiful, but grimly or antagonistically so, as if she regarded her looks as a gift she'd been unable to decline or destroy. She opened the door and swung around to face me. Her blond hair fell loosely over the collar of a plaid shirt. She wore faded jeans and rested her scuffed brown leather boots on the truck's running board.

"Where do you want to talk?" she asked.

"Probably not across from my bedroom window."

"You didn't tell your wife?"

"What's there to tell?"

I retreated a step and turned in the direction of the park. Ruta swept her purse off the seat, hopped down and shut the door. We walked wordlessly to the bench I'd occupied while waiting for her.

Once we'd sat, she rummaged in her purse for a cigarette and a lighter. Sparking the flame, she said, "I hope you're not expecting me to jerk you off or anything."

"It hadn't crossed my mind," I said.

"Really?" she replied mordantly, and lit her cigarette. "I was in Alberta for almost ten years working in the oil sands. You probably read all sorts of shit about it. Most of it was true. Guys propositioned me all the time. Not just me, but any woman with a pulse. In the work camps and on the job sites, you could be offered hundreds or even thousands of dollars to jerk someone off or blow them. It could be the labourers, the cooks, the security guards, the supervisors, oil executives, even cops. I never did, in case you're wondering. Not because I'm a prude or a feminist or anything, but because I respect myself and demand to be respected for what I can do. Which is a lot more than jerking people off."

To substantiate her point, Ruta rifled through her purse for her phone and showed me photographs similar to the one I'd seen in her mother's kitchen: her beside or inside large machines. As she swiped through the images, I noted that she had exceptionally well-formed hands, the fingers long and slender, though the nails were trimmed or bitten to the quick. There was also something manic about the play of her hands that seeped increasingly into the pitch of her voice. She lingered on a shot she'd taken through the windshield of an excavator depicting the colossal raw expanses of the bitumen mines. Her job had been to clear the land of overburden—layers of worthless rock and dirt that rested atop the valuable resource. She proudly displayed a series of pictures of a trailer home she'd bought. She'd been paid handsomely for her work but had sunk much of her money into the trailer at the peak of the market. Then the price of oil tanked and work became precarious. And then, in the spring, the wildfire struck and reduced her home to a pile of toxic ash. She'd been forced to flee, just like her grandparents from the Red Army, snatching only a few possessions and driving her truck through the flames. The only refuge she could afford while waiting for the insurance company to process her claim—which they were in no hurry to do—was in her mother's house. Ironically, it was a desire to escape her mother's house and seek her independence that had compelled her to go to Alberta in the first place. Now she was stranded there and even more miserable than she'd been before.

In the time she spoke, Ruta didn't provide me an opening to say a word, and I felt a growing and desperate need to leave—as if for the sake of my sanity. I sensed that I had finally arrived at the stage Knut had warned me about, and I feared that anything Ruta might say about my grandfather—true or false—would do me harm. I'd pursued the mystery faithfully and lovingly, but it was clear to me now that people either didn't know, wouldn't say or couldn't be trusted to speak sense.

I rose from the bench and said something to this effect as diplomatically as I could.

Ruta responded with a look of naked, childlike hurt—a look that declared that I'd joined the ranks of all the people who'd disappointed her in life.

"I was trying to form a human connection," she said. "But if you can't handle that kind of intimacy, I'm not going to force it on you. I respect your choice. But it doesn't change my intentions. I came here to repay my family's debt to your grandfather and to Jewish people."

Once more she dug into her purse and this time pulled out a sealed, white letter-size envelope, which she then extended to me.

"You can do what you want with it. Open it. Don't open it. Throw it into one of the garbage cans with the diapers and dog shit. It's up to you."

I accepted it and turned to go. Ruta remained where she was, smoking her cigarette. But before I'd gone very far, she called after me.

"Did my mother say anything about the child my grandmother left behind in Latvia?"

"She didn't," I said, though my tone made clear that the existence of the child wasn't a revelation to me.

"Did she show you the drawing of my grandmother's cat?"

"She did."

"Did you happen to ask why she took her fucking cat and not her child?"

It would have been impossible to ask, but I felt stupid that it hadn't even occurred to me.

"My grandmother was very beautiful and very weak. My grandfather ruled her life. If he decided they weren't going to take her Jewish bastard, then guess what, her Jewish bastard got left behind."

Ruta looked at me defiantly, as if, having dangled such provocative bait, she dared me to keep walking. I felt a shiver of disdain pass through me.

I held up the envelope. "What's in it?"

"Our family history."

"I know about it."

"Then you know about it," she replied.

In reproach, I tore the envelope open where I stood. It contained a single photocopy, which I read by the light of my phone. One side was a typed and notarized document in Latvian; the other side bore a handwritten English translation.

> *I, Berls Singers, born in Baltinava, Latvia, the sole surviving heir of my parents, Natans and Fruma Singers, declare that my family was dispossessed of property by the Soviet occupiers in the form of two houses at 7 and 20 Darza Street and a leather store at 5 Tirgus Street. I assert my rights to have the properties restored to me and their deeds*

*transferred to Mara Smiltnieks, my biological daughter
from Lauma Gulbis, née Smiltnieks.
Signed this 17th day of February 2001 in Toronto, Canada.*

I looked up to find Ruta eyeing me boldly, as if we were now implicitly joined in profound and painful feeling.

"My mother was never going to tell you."

The anger I'd felt drained away and was replaced by a weary pity.

"To protect Mara? So I didn't go after the houses and the store?"

"You had a right to know."

I walked slowly back to the bench and sat beside her.

"We knew, but we believed she was my grandfather's brother's."

"Not according to what your grandfather wrote here."

"If he wrote it out of charity, better to write *daughter* rather than *niece*. There's nobody left to deny it."

"You're denying it."

"Ruta, it doesn't matter," I said. "It's all past. You can believe whatever you want."

"Thanks, so can you."

"I try not to believe what I want to believe."

"I don't understand," she said with exasperation. "Why did you even text me?"

"I don't know. I thought there would be more."

She reached into her purse again for cigarettes. Deliberately averting her eyes from me, she lit one and gazed out at the park.

I reflected on the tortuous circumstances that had brought us together. Something had happened a long time ago between people who were no longer alive and whom we would be the last to know. For flawed and powerful reasons, we assigned too much importance to it, even as we didn't really know what it was.

Had our grandparents loved each other but suppressed their feelings for the sake of the brother with the dent in his head? Had they coveted each other, as proscribed by the Bible? Or had they simply, in the terror-eros of war, submitted to a spontaneous passion?

Through green fields, insuperable Aryans advanced. Of one hundred Jewish families in Baltinava, three fled. The others perished. Perhaps at Ruta's grandfather's hand. In the shadow of the crimson reckoning, Lauma looked into her daughter's face for the last time and left.

On my phone were pictures I'd taken of my girls at Georgian Bay. They posed in their swimsuits on the white sand, in the glare of the sun; the dark, shallow lake spread out behind them, stands of birch and pine describing the coast. The setting evoked the summers I'd spent as a boy on the Baltic shore. My memory of them now was visceral and ephemeral, like a deep breath. I brought up the photos and offered them to Ruta. She took the phone from my hand and studied them carefully. From across the park, a girl shrieked. The sound whisked through the night like an arrow that landed between us, narrowly missing its mark. Ruta and I startled and looked to each other as if we might embrace or leap to each other's defence. The sincerity of the feeling gripped us and then released as the girl's shriek spiralled into laughter.

Childhood

As a treat, on the way to the appointment, they stopped at an Indian restaurant, and Mark Berman listened to his son pronounce the items on the menu. That they had made it this far was already a feat, since it meant they'd managed to leave the house, walk down to the main street and board a bus filled with people, some of whose bodies gave off strange scents. Along the way, there had been tears, but they were mostly symbolic, the boy's means of asserting himself.

In the restaurant, Reuben was happier and behaved like a little adult, summoning the courage to glance at the waiter when he placed his order. A year before, he wouldn't have set foot in this restaurant, couldn't have been convinced to try the alien food, and would have answered the waiter by looking at the tablecloth. Some combination of time and enzymes had eased him. The boy was eight, and he was doing better.

There were lots of reasons to be optimistic. He was a proficient reader in both English and French. He could amuse himself for hours, concocting stories and creating intricate drawings. He remembered the lyrics to seemingly every song he'd ever heard and, using his index fingers, could tease their melodies out on the piano. He was physically robust and could swim and ice-skate and do karate. Sometimes, boys from his class invited him to their houses; other times, they invited themselves over to his. Mark would encounter them in the kitchen—funny, eager boys named for English monarchs and biblical prophets—opening cupboards in search of snacks. But many mornings, when he dropped his son at school, he'd see these same boys in a fizzy little scrum and his son tentative to approach, lurking on the periphery, gazing absently about, with none of them taking note of him. There were also fits of temper. A relentless argumentativeness. Extreme sensitivities to sense phenomena—a phantom smell in the car, dishes with unsightly patterns, the textures of clothing. Mutating phobias—of the bin under the sink for the kitchen waste, a malevolence in a tree at the playground, getting caught outside in the rain. And absent-mindedness—lost shoes and lunch boxes, perpetually forgotten homework—and an otherworldly spaciness, minutes like eons when he stood holding his underpants while reading a book he'd read before.

Mark didn't know what to make of it. Did it fall within the margin of error? What constituted ordinary childhood? What did they have to go on? Report cards were composed in a language that bore only a faint resemblance to English. Parent-teacher conferences had the polite, anxious feel of second dates. Then there was the hysterical Internet. Contrast with his older sister. Comparison against Mark's imperfect memories of his own childhood. Did he have even a single distinct memory of himself at eight? Everything before—what, twelve?—felt like a brown haze punctuated by bright spectra of embarrassment or shame. Here the object of cruelty, there the subject of boastfulness, of pettiness, of deceit. He vacillated between thinking he had been just like and nothing like him. So he and his wife had put off making the appointment until it felt just too irresponsible and cowardly not to. Then they put it off some more. Until, in a spasm of conviction— the way they accomplished most things—Mark phoned the office and set a date.

They finished their meal and rose from the table, now with only a short walk between them and the appointment. He expected his son to grow wary and sullen, but he acted as if he'd forgotten how much he had dreaded this day. Instead, he basked in the glow of having eaten a challenging, sophisticated meal.

"It was really spicy," he said. "It was even too spicy for you."

. . . .

On the street, there was construction—the city was digging a new subway line—and sidewalks were barricaded, requiring pedestrians to walk along narrow pathways and cross at improvised intersections. Confused drivers weren't sure where to stop. Without Mark asking, Reuben slipped his soft, slightly damp hand into his. Mark could count the number of times his son had done that. For the first five, six years of his life, he hadn't liked anyone but his mother to touch him. At a certain point, by way of compromise, the boy would let Mark lay his hand on his cheek and then kiss it to say good night. But now he held Mark's hand and prattled on about some incident at school. Something "gross" a boy in his class had done. Then about his part in a social studies project on Manitoba. Did Mark know about polar bears in Churchill? Which reminded him of a riddle Elijah, his project partner, had told him about a cowboy who rides into town on Friday and leaves three days later on Friday. (His horse's name was Friday!) For a moment, Mark interpreted his son's chattiness as a sign that he'd stopped being nervous about the appointment. Then, thinking deeper, he realized that it actually meant the opposite. A more astute, sensitive father would have understood this right away. His son had taken his hand because he was very nervous and was talking compulsively to mask his fear. Why he didn't understand this immediately, why his son so often seemed like a mystery to him, felt like a personal failing. He pictured the trunk of a tall, broad oak. This was how a father's love should be. His was wrapped in creeping vines.

....

After navigating more barricades and obstacles, they found the entrance to the medical building where the avenue made a weird jog, terminating and then continuing a block to the west. The building was of a kind popularized in the 1960s, brown, brutalist and not very inviting. Mark normally wouldn't care, but he knew his son would. It couldn't help that they were going into an ugly building. He had the address and all the details but still consulted the directory, also of the period— white plastic letters pressed into a black plastic board. He found the name and suite numbers: Dr. C. Katsenelenbogen 203, 204.

They climbed one flight of stairs and approached room 203. A small, hand-written card tacked to the door informed: *If the door is locked, please go to room 204.* The handle gave way, and they entered a small reception room that had no provision for a receptionist. He noted two upholstered chairs, in a mid-century modern style, flanking a pale maple end table stacked with children's books and juvenile magazines. Beyond the reception area were two rooms, one whose door was shut, the other whose door was open. Unsure what to do, they didn't make any deliberate sounds to announce themselves. But, through the open door, a woman appeared anyway. She smiled and offered her hand and introduced herself as Dr. Claire Katsenelenbogen but asked that they call her Claire. She was slightly older than Mark, of less than average height, dressed in a neutral caftan-style blouse and matching slacks, her dark curls gathered in a loose knot atop

her head. She had neat, regular features, which had probably always suited her, was sufficiently but not exceedingly
pretty, so as not to detract from her brains. Something about
her seemed familiar, which wasn't unusual in the fishbowl of
Jewish Toronto. She could have been the older sister of a forgotten high-school friend. Or maybe just the representative
of a certain social type: the daughter of a progressive mother
and a father with a good head for business.

She opened the door to the room where she conducted her
client meetings. A window overlooked the street and framed
a steel desk. Claire seated herself behind the desk, and Mark
took the seat across from her. Beside him was another chair
and beside that, at the corner of the desk, was a red synthetic
fur beanbag chair. His son weighed his options and, resentful of being watched, turned his back to Mark and knelt on
the beanbag, averting his face from Claire as well.

"Reuben," he admonished, though he knew it would be
less than futile, produce the counter-effect.

His son plucked at the fur and fixated on a spot between
the top of the beanbag and a bookshelf on the nearest wall.
*Brain Lateralization of Children, Beyond Freedom and Dignity,
The Psychology of Sex Differences, Precocity and Perversity*
and *Children and Arson* were among the happy titles.

"Reuben, do you know why you're here?" Claire asked.

"Because I forget things," his son replied uncertainly.

"What kinds of things?"

"My agenda from school and stuff like that."

"Does it bother you when you forget things?"

"Sometimes," his son said, and squinted at some red fibres that had stuck to his fingers.

"And do you know what we're going to do here today?"

"Tests?"

"Kinds of tests. Some questions have right answers and some don't. You'll just do your best, okay?"

His son nodded, and Claire slid a thick manila envelope over to Mark.

"Your mom and dad will answer some questions too. It'll be their homework." She delivered this rote little quip with a dry smile, so as not to insult anyone's intelligence.

Inside the envelope were two identical sets of workbooks, six in total. Each workbook concerned itself with a related but slightly different set of capacities and behaviours. They'd notice some overlap in the questions, but this was intentional. Completing each workbook would take anywhere from fifteen minutes to half an hour. Some questions they'd be able to answer instantly; others would require reflection. Parents were meant to complete one set of workbooks, with the other set to be completed by the child's schoolteacher. Once all were done, the data could be compiled and integrated with the results of his son's testing. They'd get a detailed report with recommendations about how to proceed. Which might include doing nothing at all.

While Claire went through this explanation, his son looked up from his hands and studied the room. There were the bookshelves to inspect, the view out the window (from that angle, little more than the tops of buildings and the white midday sky) and some diplomas and lithographs on classical Japanese themes—a pink lily, a snow-capped mountain. The name on the diplomas was Claire Gelb.

Mark tried to remember how he knew the name Claire Gelb as he sat in the waiting area of room 204 while, in another room, Claire administered a more systematic memory test to his son.

"Say the numbers back to me in reverse order: 9, 1."

"1, 9."

"4, 5, 8."

"8, 5, 4."

"7, 5, 4, 2."

"2, 5, 4, 7."

"2, 1, 7, 9, 4."

"4, 9, 2 . . ."

"It's all right. 6, 3, 7, 2, 9, 1?"

"1, 9, 2, 7, 3, 6?"

"Very good. And can you say these numbers back in numerical order, smallest to biggest? 7, 5, 8, 1."

"1, 5, 7, 8."

Mark attempted the questions along with his son and didn't do nearly as well. One day, he imagined, he'd be given this same test to establish just how much his mind had deteriorated.

In another room, its door open, another psychologist put a different set of questions to someone else's child.

"Please define *island*. What does *ancient* mean? How many hours are in a day? Name something in space not made by humans. Why is it important to tell the truth? How could stress be a good thing? What are problems with rapid changes in science and technology? What does the heart do?"

Every answer was like wiping a little more of the murk from the future. *This is what is inside you. It is your potential. People rarely transcend. Even if you are granted love and support,* X *awaits you. Probably more like* X *minus* Y.

Moved by boredom, curiosity and foreboding, Mark opened one of the workbooks and read the questions. They were written in plain language and arranged in neat columns, the diligent work of confirmed specialists—researchers, editors, publishers—that made undeniably and pitiably real the agonies people were living in their homes each day. The answers were graded on a scale that started with "Not at all," proceeded to "Just a little," "Pretty much," and then dropped into the abyss of "Very much."

- Picks at things (nails, fingers, hair, clothing)
- Problems with making or keeping friends
- Excitable, impulsive
- Cries easily or often
- Daydreams
- Difficulty learning

- Restless in the "squirmy" sense
- Fearful (of new situations, people, places, school)
- Restless, always up and on the go
- Problems with eating
- Bowel problems
- Destructive
- Shy
- Quarrelsome
- Pouts and sulks
- Feels lonely, unwanted or unloved
- Fails to finish things
- Mood changes quickly and drastically
- Harms others (pets, friends, siblings)
- Harms self
- Doesn't understand/respect other people's physical and sexual boundaries
- Plays with own genitals
- Basically an unhappy child

It was then that he remembered how he knew Claire. She'd been the host of a local television program when he was a boy. The show aired every afternoon after school and consisted of her answering questions about relationships and sex. She would have been in her early twenties, not all that much older than her callers. It was the mid-1980s, before the great disgorgement, when the world still seemed full of intimate, hidden things. Under the cover of the show, kids unburdened themselves while other kids watched giddily or silently in their living rooms and basements.

Mark usually watched with other Russian kids, whose parents had bought homes in a modest development within sight of the apartment buildings where they'd landed not long before, penniless and bewildered. They were boys and girls often left to their own devices, pulled daily into the evolving drama of the street. They called each other friends, but it was friendship marred by intrigue, jealousy, mockery and distrust. He didn't know why it was like that. Maybe it was immigrant. Maybe it was Soviet.

When he was twelve or thirteen, in a misguided attempt at fellowship, he revealed a vulnerability, and like sadistic little ogres, they tormented him. He could have said, "The whole world is beating off," but that was still privileged information. He had never before known such misery. No day passed without ridicule and the threat of exposure. They would drop hints in front of strangers. There was something the matter with him. He was deviant. For his own good, they would tell his parents.

Alone, he suffered and prayed that they would tire of persecuting him. He could see no way to make them stop. He suffered and masturbated, the pleasure just barely exceeding the shame. He hunched on the toilet with a page from a pornographic magazine, of a woman in high heels presenting herself from behind. He hadn't hit puberty and there were functions his body couldn't yet perform, but she had already imprinted herself on his erotic life. He would lock the door and, heart pounding, pinch the tiny exposed corner of the photograph from where it protruded between the bathroom mirror and the wall. And then fold it up and slide it back into its hiding place, careful not to push it in so far that he wouldn't be able to retrieve it again.

Then, one day, someone proposed the hilarious idea to call the TV show on behalf of a friend who had a problem. Red-faced and on the verge of tears, he ran home and, out of inchoate desperation and hate, called the show himself. It was the closest he'd come to wishing he were dead.

His son emerged from the room where he'd been tested and came over to him looking mildly disconcerted, as if he wasn't sure quite what to be upset about.

"Finished?" Mark asked.

"I have a break before the next test."

He stood by Mark's side and his expression altered slightly, as if a source of frustration had revealed itself.

"What is it?"

"You're probably going to say no."

"Always possible."

He shifted in place and said, "Can I play a game on your phone?"

Mark gave him his phone and got up to give him his seat as well. The boy curled up, resting his chin on his knees, and abandoned himself to the screen so that he didn't notice or mind Mark looking at him. When he was untroubled, he was quite a handsome boy. Of his two children, his son was the one who looked at all like him. In the set of Reuben's chin and the shape of his mouth, Mark also glimpsed his own father, who'd died before the boy was born. Mark couldn't say why that should matter. It shouldn't matter. Only it was evident that something of his resided in his son.

Claire came out of the testing room and walked purposefully toward the door that led to the hallway. She and Mark exchanged a polite smile as she passed. She opened the door, stepped partway out and then turned back.

"I've been trying to remember where I know you from," she said and loosed a flush of panic in him as if, because he had been thinking about her, she could read his thoughts. "Is your family Russian?"

"Actually, Latvian. Soviet," he bumbled. "But basically Russian."

"My husband's family is Russian. I think your parents were at our wedding."

"Your in-laws, what are their names?" he asked, but he didn't recognize them.

"My associate will do the other testing," Claire said as she turned to go. "The language and concepts."

Unable to stop himself, he followed her out into the hall, startling her.

"I remember you too."

"Oh," she said.

"You must hear that a lot."

"How is that?"

"From your show," he said.

He saw her expression assume a professional opacity, as if the mode between them had abruptly changed. Perhaps, he thought, he had reminded her of a former self she no longer identified with. It was such a long time ago, and she had been so young. Or maybe she really didn't know what he was talking about. He'd confused her with an entirely different person. Descending further, he started to question whether he had misremembered the whole thing. There hadn't been a show.

"Your son is very sweet," Claire said to break the silence.

"He did okay?"

"He did fine."

"Do you think he'll be all right?"

"Most of us turn out all right," she said with calm finality.

He felt the ludicrous urge to insist and say, *I called you and you saved my life*, but she had gone, and anyway, it was beside the point.

Roman's Song

ROMAN BERMAN LOOKED AGAIN at his rectangular desk clock, a complimentary gift that had come with the first *Time* magazine subscription. The subscription ran him sixty dollars a year, but he justified it as a necessary expense. Even though he planned his schedule meticulously and rarely kept a patient waiting, the magazines lent his office a sense of professionalism. Though he preferred the newspaper, he sometimes perused the magazines himself—particularly if there was a profile of an athlete or a businessman. Other times, if he came across something that he thought would be of interest to his son, he brought the magazine home. Recently, there had been an article about a famous Hollywood movie director, the son of Hungarian Jews. The director had immigrated with his parents to America when he was a boy of six, like his own son. He had then gone on to attain tremendous success. The article described him as a millionaire many times over. Roman wondered if his son had read it. He'd brought it home the previous week. He made a mental note to ask his son when he got home. Not to pressure him, of course, only to inquire.

It was 5:20 and Svirsky was now more than half an hour late. Roman had specifically told Svirsky to come to the office at 4:30, after his last patient of the day. But at 4:30 there had been no sign of Svirsky. Roman had been surprised. If he had been in Svirsky's position, not only would he have been on time, he would have been early. But apparently Svirsky didn't think this way. Roman waited and tried to sort his files, but he found it nearly impossible to focus and frequently consulted the clock. He himself always tried to be punctual. On the rare occasion when he was detained, he made sure to call and alert his appointment. Svirsky hadn't called. It infuriated Roman, especially since he was the one doing Svirsky a favour.

Earlier that week Roman had gotten a call from Lyona Ribak, Svirsky's brother-in-law. At first Roman thought Lyona was calling about the status of his insurance claim, but Lyona didn't mention the claim. He asked about Roman's Volvo.

"I was going to put an ad in the paper," Roman said.

"How does it run?" Lyona asked.

"Very well. It leaks a little oil, but I top it up once a week."

"Renata's brother just came here from Leningrad."

"She must be happy."

"She can be happy, the problems come down on my head."

"He needs a car?"

"He has a car. Against my advice he bought a Ford Tempo. Used. A piece of garbage. Some mornings it starts, some mornings it doesn't start. You could flip a coin. He has two kids, one and seven. The wife is at home with the baby. I found him a job at a scrapyard, but without a car he can't get to work."

Roman had been sympathetic. After all, it wasn't that long since he had been in Svirsky's shoes. Nobody needed to remind him how little separated him from Svirsky. An outsider might see his office and presume that everything had fallen into place, but Roman knew better. He lived from phone call to phone call. Come the holidays he made the rounds of doctors' offices, bringing a bottle of cognac or a box of chocolates, doing what he could to ensure that they didn't forget about him and kept referring their patients. The receptionists weren't always happy to see him; some ignored him and made him wait. "Hi, Shirley." "Hi, Wanda." "Happy Hanukkah, Racquel." It was no great joy to go simpering around like that, but he was prepared to do it if it paid the overhead, the mortgage and what they charged for Hebrew school. Every now and then, when a big jackpot was announced, he bought a lottery ticket, but he didn't hold out any hopes of becoming rich. He was a man who had come to a new country in his forties, with few marketable skills, equipped with no English apart from two novelty phrases: "Life is very complicated" and "Keep in touch." In his more sanguine moments, Roman thought: Anything I've attained, I should feel fortunate.

In light of this he'd consented to help Lyona. He assured him that his brother-in-law would get a decent car at a fair price. True, Roman thought, you invited trouble whenever you did business with friends. The Volvo could break down tomorrow and then there would be bad feelings. With a stranger you could wash your hands of the thing, but with a friend you assumed responsibilities. Nevertheless, he agreed to do it. He even refrained from putting the ad in the newspaper. But now, for all his good intentions, he was sitting around like a fool.

Roman considered waiting another ten minutes, until 5:30, before going home. It wasn't often that he was able to get home so early. Usually, he had appointments until after six. He didn't get in until seven or later. By then his wife and son would have already eaten dinner. The boy might be doing homework, reading or watching television. Roman would eat alone and maybe spend a few minutes with his son between television shows, before the boy went to sleep. He wanted to stay involved in his son's life, to be a good father to him. But it was a difficult age; the boy was often moody and irritable and made Roman feel as if he disapproved of him, as if Roman was always putting an emphasis on all the wrong things.

Roman resolved to go. But at that moment he heard the jangling of the bell on his front door. Now, finally, here was this Svirsky, Roman thought. He'd accumulated so much resentment waiting for him that he felt tempted to turn him away and teach him a lesson. Well, that he wouldn't do, but he would certainly vent his displeasure. The mere thought of venting his displeasure made Roman feel better. He was eager for Svirsky to come through the door and into the inner room where Roman had his file cabinets and his desk.

"In here," Roman called.

But it wasn't Svirsky who came through the door. When he saw who it was, Roman cursed both himself and Svirsky. He should have left earlier, he knew it. He had tried to do some-one a good turn and now, inevitably, he was being punished.

"We were passing by and thought we'd stop in to see if you were busy," Kopman said.

With him was his partner, Gruber, the Israeli. Gruber fol-lowed after Kopman and then stepped aside to make room for an attractive young woman. She had straight brown hair down to her shoulders, and wore pink lipstick and pale, whitish eye makeup. She was tall for a woman; in heels she was level with Kopman. She was also slim, but in a tight blouse and short skirt everything she had was exhibited to maximum effect.

Since he rarely had occasion to meet with more than one person at a time, Roman had only two chairs on the opposite side of his desk.

"It looks like we caught you at a good time," Kopman said, before sitting in one of the chairs.

"I was waiting for someone. He's late. I was about to leave."

"Good then," Kopman said. "We'll only be a minute."

Kopman motioned for the woman to sit in the second vacant chair. He spoke to her in English.

"Sit, Felicia, dear."

The woman did as she was told and sat almost directly across from Roman. She gazed at the wall, at a spot vaguely above Roman's right shoulder. There he had his framed diploma from the Board of Directors of Masseurs, a recent school picture of his son, and an arts and crafts project the boy had done years ago in summer camp—a pattern of nails strung with green yarn that spelled out the Hebrew word *Shalom*.

"Well," Kopman said, "we just wanted to know if you'd given more thought to our proposition."

Roman looked from Kopman to Gruber, who stood behind him, and made no effort to mask his feelings about their proposition. He didn't like either of them. Gruber was antsy and unhealthy. He was obese and careless about his personal appearance. He had a thick growth of stubble, and his kinky hair bulged like stuffing from the baseball cap that he'd neglected to remove. Kopman, Roman's wife had known as a girl in Rezekne. They had been in the same class. After he graduated from high school, his family left for Israel. All kinds of stories circulated about what he'd gotten himself involved in over there. Roman's wife hadn't even heard that he'd come to Toronto until he'd shown up unexpectedly at Roman's office.

The first time, just the two of them had come, Kopman and Gruber. They'd arrived in the evening while Roman was with a patient. When the door rang, Roman had stepped into the waiting room to investigate, since he'd had no more patients scheduled and wasn't expecting anyone. Kopman had introduced himself, mentioned his old acquaintance with Roman's wife and said that he was there with a business proposition. What proposition? Why arrive unannounced? Kopman didn't explain. Roman hadn't liked the look of the two of them from the beginning, and he'd had a hard time concentrating on finishing the session with his patient. When the patient left, Roman had had no choice but to allow Kopman and Gruber to outline their proposition.

Their proposition amounted to this: they were pimps and they wanted to make him into a pimp too.

There was good money to be made in massage parlours, Kopman said; all they needed was someone with a valid masseur's licence. Other than supplying his licence, Roman wouldn't have to do anything. They would take care of everything. They would set up the business and manage it. Once a month Roman would receive a cheque with a percentage of the profits. He wouldn't have to so much as lift a finger. If the first parlour proved successful, they could expand.

"And if the police come?" Roman asked.

"If the police come we try to arrive at an arrangement," Kopman said.

"And if they don't accept your arrangement?"

"Then they will just close the place down," Kopman said.

"And report me and revoke my licence," Roman said.

"You might get a warning, that's all," Kopman said. "You know how many places like this there are in the city?"

"Enough," Roman said.

"So why shouldn't you benefit also? Do you deserve any less? I'm sure it wasn't easy to write the exams and get the licence," Kopman said. "If it was easy, I wouldn't be here. I'd do it myself."

Roman had told them that he wasn't interested. They had suggested that he reconsider.

"Why rush to refuse?" Kopman asked. "There's real money to be made. Take some time. Think about it. It's a good opportunity."

In the days that followed, Roman had repeated the conversation to his brother-in-law and to a few select friends. All had been of the opinion that he should explore further. They'd heard of such enterprises. It was no lie, people made money. Besides, what was so horrible about a massage parlour? If Roman decided to go ahead with it, nobody would condemn him.

Despite what they said, Roman had misgivings. Kopman was right, passing the exam hadn't been easy. He had devoted himself to it for more than a year. After a day of warehouse work, he had come home to study. In all his life he had never worked so hard. All the while he had been sustained by dreams of opening his own practice, being his own boss, providing for his family in a dignified way. He lived that year in a state of perpetual anxiety. He was tyrannized by the fear that he would fail the exam and be consigned forever to a life of warehouse labour. No matter how long and gruelling the hours of study, they paled against the wretched prospect of failure. When he received the letter informing him that he had passed, he was jubilant. He felt that he had accomplished something monumental. He would work in a clean office, almost like a doctor, and his son wouldn't have to be ashamed of him.

He'd spent seven years building a good reputation. He had devoted clients who ascribed to him their miraculous recoveries. An old man who couldn't get out of bed, now walked to buy his groceries. An accountant who couldn't tie his shoes, now played tennis. An arthritic grandmother who couldn't turn a doorknob, now planted roses and baked cookies. He'd dealt honestly with people. He'd never cheated anyone. Whatever he did was within the law, or, if it exceeded, it wasn't in any odious way. He did what everybody did to stay in business. If somebody had a benefits plan that covered massage, he'd provide a document attesting to treatment and then split the proceeds. If somebody got into a car accident, he would diagnose an injury to assist with the insurance claim. It was because of this that Lyona Ribak, for instance, stood to collect $2,400. There was nothing contemptible about it. Benefits money, if left unused, disappeared; and each year, the insurance companies, renowned crooks, made billions in profits.

But to become involved with people like Kopman and Gruber and to risk his reputation for a brothel was something entirely different. The worst kind of trouble could happen in such a place. There could be drugs, fights, even murder. If anything happened, he could be implicated, sent to prison. He imagined the scandal and the humiliation. How could he face his wife and son? And even if nothing happened, what if his son discovered that he'd become a partner in a brothel? How would he explain such a sordid thing? More money? This was no explanation. They weren't starving. Without a massage parlour, he and his wife had jobs and were doing okay.

He would rather struggle and live modestly than gamble and lead that kind of life. He'd already experienced that kind of life. His father had lived that way. When they settled in Riga after the evacuation, his father had traded on the black market. He had speculated in gold, gemstones, textiles and heirlooms. Officially, his job was as fire marshal at a theatre, but he was there only during performances, a few evenings a week. The rest of the time he was free to pursue deals. They were a family of five: Roman, his parents and his two sisters. His mother stayed home and looked after the house. The situation after the war was grim, sections of the city were rubble and there were shortages of everything. His father bore a heavy burden. He was a small, austere man, frugal in his affections, but Roman revered him. Roman was twelve, thirteen, fourteen, at the time, the same age as his own son now. He hadn't known every detail, but he'd known enough about how his father made his living. Once, his father had woken him in the middle of the night, taken him into the cellar and showed him where he had hidden a box containing gold coins and banknotes. In case something happens, his father had said.

Roman understood that if the authorities ever caught him, his father would be severely punished. Almost certainly he would be sent far away, where anything could befall him. He worried also about the people with whom his father associated and the harm they might do him. Nights when his father was late coming home, Roman didn't sleep. He snuck outside and stood in the shadowy passageway that led from their building's courtyard to Red Army Street. There he stood and peered into the night until he saw his father's familiar form walking resolutely home. The sight always made him dumb with relief, gratitude and love. Though when his father saw him, he became furious and berated him for lurking about and drawing attention. But no matter how many times his father berated him, Roman couldn't help it. He couldn't sleep or keep still. He had to go out to the street, because every second of not-knowing was unbearable. And once he saw his father, the abuse didn't matter, because his father was home.

Roman did not want to subject his son to that kind of life.

To Kopman he said, "I thought about it. I talked to people. But I haven't changed my opinion. It's not for me. I'm not interested."

"It really is a shame you feel that way," Kopman said. "Personally, I think you have the wrong idea about what we are suggesting."

"What wrong idea? I understand everything perfectly well."

"Have you ever visited such a place?"

"What the hell for?" Roman said.

"Some of the places are dirty. Maybe you think we would be running a dirty place?"

"Kopman," Roman said, "I don't care what kind of place you plan to run."

"The place will be nice," Gruber said in English. "We would only make a nice place."

"This is why we brought Felicia," Kopman said. "So that you could see for yourself the kind of girl we would hire."

At the mention of her name, Felicia glanced opaquely from Kopman to Roman.

"Stand up, Felicia, dear," Kopman said. "Let Roman take a look at you."

Obediently, Felicia pushed her chair back and rose. She didn't make any lewd poses or change the expression on her face. She stood with her hands at her sides and rested her weight slightly on one hip.

"You see what a beautiful girl," Kopman said. "Guess how old."

"What are you doing, Kopman?" Roman said.

"Twenty-three," Kopman said. "She isn't just some whore off the street. She's very intelligent. You can talk to her. Ask her where she's from."

"It makes no difference to me where she's from," Roman said.

"She's Czech. From Prague," Kopman said. "Where are you from, Felicia?"

Speaking in a bored, faraway voice, the girl said, "I'm from Prague."

Kopman raised his eyebrows and smiled triumphantly, as if he had proved a disputed point.

"She's also educated," Kopman said. "She has a medical background. In Czechoslovakia she studied to be a nurse. She knows massage. She's not a professional like you, of course, but she's very good."

"Fine. Is that all? Are you finished?" Roman said.

"You don't believe me?" Kopman asked. "Take her into the other room. Tell her what you like. She'll do anything you say."

"Kopman," Roman said, "what's wrong with you? You grew up with my wife. You went to school together."

"Yes? So? She was a good student. She helped me with my homework. What does one thing have to do with the other?"

"Get out of my office. Get out," Roman said.

"Don't be rash," Kopman said.

Roman turned his attention to the girl. She looked like a normal girl. She was no different from anyone you saw on the street. He wondered how she had become like this. How had she gotten mixed up with scum like Kopman and Gruber?

"Young lady," Roman said.

She lowered her eyes and looked at him, slightly confused, as if uncertain that he had addressed her.

"Young lady," Roman said. "I read in the newspaper that there are not enough nurses. You studied to be a nurse. Go away from these guys. Hospitals are looking for nurses. Go be a nurse."

A hard, unpleasant look crossed the girl's face.

"Fuck you," she said.

With that, they left.

What a miserable day, Roman thought as he drove home. It was already six o'clock. After Kopman, Gruber and the girl had left, he'd taken several minutes to compose himself. He was plagued by a bad feeling, like he had been soiled. He also found it hard to banish the image of the girl's cruel face. He'd meant only to be kind, and her viciousness had taken him completely by surprise. He felt her insult keenly, like a slap.

He steered the Volvo up Bathurst, to Finch, turned on Torresdale, and into his subdivision. Six o'clock and not a word from that bastard Svirsky, Roman thought. A miserable day.

Roman parked the car in the driveway and climbed the cement steps of his porch. When he unlocked the front door, he sensed something odd. It took him a moment to register what it was. He saw a pair of strange boots in the entryway, worn and scuffed. Then he heard his wife's voice coming from the kitchen, speaking politely, even formally. After this he heard a man's voice, thanking her, declining something, in a muted, timid way. Roman didn't call out to announce his arrival but went up to the kitchen, where he saw a man

seated at the table, his back to him. The man was still wearing his jacket. Seated across from him was Roman's wife. A
teapot, cups, fruits and biscuits were on the table. Beyond
the kitchen, in the living room, the television was on, and his
son was lying on the sofa.

"There you are, Roman," his wife said when he entered.
This caused the man to turn in his chair to face him. Intro-
ductions were unnecessary, but his wife identified him as
Edik Svirsky.

Svirsky looked to be in his middle thirties, with a haggard
though handsome face. His eyes were gentle, brown and
filled—as the saying went—with all the sorrow of the Jewish
people. His hair, like a boy's, peaked in the middle. He was
thin, but his hands, which fidgeted nervously, were large and
strong, the nails dirty from the scrapyard.

"We just called you at the office, but you had already
gone," his wife said.

She shifted a cup and a saucer and bid Roman to sit down.

Roman didn't sit but said, "Of course I'd gone. I'd been
waiting since 4:30."

He stared at Svirsky, expecting an explanation. The scru-
tiny made Svirsky fidget even more.

"His car broke down," his wife said.

"I'm very sorry," Svirsky said. "I wanted to call but I couldn't
find your number. I was at work; they'd agreed to let me leave
early. But the car wouldn't start. Guys from work tried to fix
it; then they called a tow truck. My English isn't very good

and I didn't understand everything that was happening. The tow truck driver took the car to the garage, but I didn't want him to. I imagined it would cost a lot to repair. I asked the driver to take it to the parking spot at my building. It was already late then. I called Lyona and he told me to just walk to your house. I hurried, but it took twenty minutes."

In the living room the television erupted in loud, idiotic laughter. It put Roman's nerves on edge, and he shouted for his son to turn it down.

"Sit," his wife said.

Roman squeezed in and sat.

His wife then called for their son to get up from the sofa and join them in the kitchen.

"Your father came home," his wife said, "come over and say hello."

His son turned off the television. He rose from the sofa as if it was a great chore. Roman watched him come. When his son had been younger, he'd been athletic. They had enrolled him in soccer in the summer and hockey in the winter. He hadn't been an exceptional player, but he had enjoyed it. And Roman had enjoyed attending the games. In his own youth he'd been something of an athlete, and he had liked having this in common with his son. But over the last year or so, his son had ceased to show much interest in sports. He'd grown his hair long in a way Roman felt didn't suit him. His complexion had suffered. He spent more time watching television or in his room reading and listening to music. Though his grades were still good, he seemed lazy and discontent. But when Roman offered a helpful suggestion, his son became sullen and withdrew.

Upon entering the kitchen, his son took the available seat beside Svirsky.

"Hi, Pa," he said automatically.

His presence at the table seemed to further unnerve Svirsky.

"I really apologize," Svirsky said. "Lyona told me not to buy that car. He recommended another. But it was more expensive, and I felt uneasy borrowing more money from him. We'd already borrowed enough. I thought if I bought the cheaper car, it would be easier on Lyona and my sister. They've been very generous. But now I know it was a big mistake. I only managed to complicate things."

"We all make mistakes." Roman shrugged.

His mood was brittle, and for some reason Svirsky's haplessness aggravated him.

"I'm very grateful to you for selling me the car," Svirsky said, and reached into his jacket pocket for an envelope.

Roman watched him fumble with it and lay it on the table. It was stout with bills.

"I took out three thousand, like we agreed," Svirsky said.

"Okay," Roman said.

With the envelope on the table, Svirsky appeared at a loss. Roman sat diagonally from him, but it seemed inappropriate to reach across the table. He expected Svirsky to pass it to him.

Svirsky, for some inexplicable reason, continued to hesitate.

"You haven't seen the car yet," Roman said. "We should go outside and I'll show you the car."

"Yes, all right," Svirsky said. But he remained tentative.

Roman pushed his chair back and got up. Svirsky, as if still hampered by something, slid his chair back slowly.

"I don't doubt you that the car is very good and worth the price," Svirsky said.

"I understand," Roman said, not quite understanding. "But I'm not offended. It's every buyer's right to inspect his car."

"The thing is," Svirsky said, "I took out three thousand dollars. And I planned to give it to you, but I didn't anticipate the charge for the tow truck."

So, finally, there it was, Roman thought.

"How much was the tow truck?" Roman asked.

"A hundred and fifty dollars," Svirsky said, penitently.

Svirsky's implication was clear and Roman looked around the table to see the reactions of his wife and son. His wife was circumspect, unwilling to provoke. But he could see that his son expected him to do the mean thing, the uncharitable thing.

"Why don't you go outside, Edik?" Roman said. "Here are the keys. Take a look at the car. Give me a few minutes to think about it."

"Yes, of course," Svirsky said, and went to tie his boots.

When Svirsky had gone, Roman looked again at his wife and son.

"Well, what do you say?" Roman asked.

"What can I say?" his wife replied.

"At three thousand dollars, the car is a good price. Maybe we could get more, but for him I didn't even put it in the newspaper."

"It's hard not to pity him," his wife said.

Roman didn't reply. He allowed for a quiet moment to prevail in which it was possible to consider and pity Svirsky. He wanted to show that he wasn't blind to the feeling. But as the moment extended, Roman believed it also allowed for a view of the complete picture. In the complete picture, Svirsky couldn't be considered alone. The complete picture also included themselves, their circumstances, their unpredictable future and the persistent, unwieldy claims of the past.

Roman rose from the table, went to the window and saw Svirsky sitting motionless in the driver's seat. His hands were in his lap and the engine was off, as if he didn't dare touch anything without permission.

"What's he doing?" Roman's wife asked.

"Sitting," Roman said.

It was easy to pity Svirsky, Roman thought. But for all his troubles, Svirsky was actually a lucky man. He possessed something Roman had lost and could never recover. Confused, tired, defeated, Svirsky would still go home to the expectant clamour of his young children. No money, no success, nothing the man attained would ever rival such joy. If he could, Roman would have traded places with Svirsky. He'd have done it in an instant, just to go back to the time when he could speak a word to his son without apprehension. To once more feel from his son a sincere, instinctive desire to be with him. He would do it just to relive the mornings when he drove his son to school. In the same Volvo that he was now selling to Svirsky. He'd do it for those fifteen minutes, when the boy sat buckled in the passenger seat. To see his small face, with its compact intelligence, a source of wonder and pride. And to watch him turn the radio dial and mouth the words to what seemed to Roman like one long, continuous song.

A New Gravestone for an Old Grave

SHORTLY BEFORE VICTOR SHULMAN was to leave on his vacation, his father called him at the office to say that Sander Rabinsky had died. From the tone of his father's voice and from the simple fact that his father had felt compelled to call him at work, Victor understood he was expected to recognize the name Sander Rabinsky and also to grasp the significance of the man's passing. Not wanting to disappoint his father by revealing his ignorance, Victor held the phone and said nothing. In recent years many of his father's friends had started to take ill and die. For the most part these were friends from his father's youth, men whom Victor could not remember, having not seen them in the twenty-five years since the Shulmans left Riga and settled in Los Angeles. For Victor they existed, if at all, in the forty-year-old photos in which they, along with his own father, appeared bare-chested and vigorous on the Baltic shore. Simka, Yashka, Vadik, Salik: athletes, womanizers and Jewish professionals, now interred in cemeteries in Calgary, New Jersey and Ramat Gan. Victor assumed that Sander Rabinsky was of the same company, although that didn't quite explain why his death merited a special phone call.

Sander Rabinsky was dead, which was of course sad, Leon Shulman explained, but there was more to it. Sander had been Leon's last remaining connection in Riga and the one Leon had entrusted with overseeing the erection of a new monument to his own father, Wolf Shulman. Of late, Leon and Sander had been in constant contact. Sander had been acting on Leon's behalf with the stonecutter and functioning as liaison with the Jewish cemetery. Leon had already wired one thousand dollars to Sander's bank, and Sander had assured Leon that a new stone would be installed in a matter of weeks. But now, with Sander's death, Leon was at a loss. With nobody there to supervise the job, he had no way of ensuring that it would be properly done.

"Believe me, I know how these things work. If nobody is standing over them, those thieves will just take the money and do nothing."

"The cemetery guy and the stonecutter?"

"There are no bigger thieves."

Little more than a year before, Leon Shulman had been forced to retire from the pharmaceutical company where he had worked for twenty-three years. The diabetes that had precipitated his own father's death had progressed to the point where it rendered Leon Shulman clinically blind. Leon was a very competent chemist, enjoyed his job and was well liked by his co-workers, but he could hardly argue when his supervisor took him aside and began enumerating the dangers posed by a blind man in a laboratory.

Since then, as his vision continued to deteriorate, Leon imposed a strict regimen upon himself. His friends were dying and he was blind: another man might have surrendered to depression, but Leon informed anyone willing to listen that he had no intention of going down that road. It wasn't that he had any illusions about mortality; he was a sick man, but sick wasn't dead. So he woke each morning at a specific hour, performed a routine of calisthenics recalled from his days in the Soviet army, dressed himself, made his own breakfast, listened to the news and then immersed himself in unfinished business. At the top of the list of unfinished business was a new gravestone for his father's grave.

On occasion, particularly when the Shulmans observed the anniversary of their arrival in Los Angeles, Leon Shulman would recount the story of his father's death. Certainly Wolf Shulman had been ill. He'd been ill for years. But the week the Shulmans were scheduled to depart, he had been no worse than he'd been in five years. Just that morning Leon had seen him and the old man had made oatmeal. So there was no way Leon could have anticipated what happened. But still, the thought that he was in a black marketeer's kitchen haggling over the price of a Kiev camera—albeit a very expensive model, with excellent optics, based on the Hasselblad—while his father was dying was something for which Leon could not forgive himself. And then the frantic preparations for the funeral, and the fact that Leon had already spent all of their money on things like the camera so that they'd have something to sell in the bazaars of Vienna and Rome made the whole cursed experience that much more unbearable. Lacking time and money, Leon grieved that he had abandoned his father, a man whom he had loved and respected, in a grave marked by a stone the size of a shoebox.

This, Victor understood, was the reason for the phone call to the office. And later that evening, after submitting himself to the indignities of rush hour on the 405 and the 101, Victor sat in the kitchen of his parents' Encino condominium and listened as his father explained how easy it would be for Victor to adjust his travel plans to include an extended weekend in Riga. Leon had already called a travel agent, a friend, who could—even on such short notice—arrange for a ticket from London to Riga. It was, after all, a direct flight. A matter of only a few hours. The same travel agent had also taken the liberty—just in case—of reserving a room for Victor at a very nice hotel in Jurmala, two minutes from the beach, near bars, restaurants and Dzintari station, where he could find a local train that would get him into Riga in a half-hour.

"Ask your mother, Jurmala in July, the beach, if the weather is good, nothing is better."

"Pa, we live in Los Angeles; if I go it won't be because of the beach."

"I didn't say because of the beach. Of course it's not because of the beach. But you'll see. The sand is like flour. The water is calm. Before you were one year old, I took you into that water. And anyway, you shouldn't worry. I'll pay for everything."

"That's right, that's my biggest worry."

When Victor had been a sophomore in college, he realized that he would need to make money. This was the same year he spent a semester abroad at Oxford—though living for three months among fledgling aristocrats had had nothing to do with his decision. For Victor, having grown up in Los Angeles, the lives and privileges of rich people—English or otherwise—were no great revelation. What led to his decision had been the first irrefutable signs of his father's declining health. It was then that Victor began driving his father to the offices of world-class specialists, experts in the pancreas, not one of whom had been able to arrest—never mind reverse—the advancement of Leon's blindness. It was then that Victor started to do the calculations that ultimately led him to law school and a position as a litigation associate at a Century City law firm. At nineteen, Victor recognized—not unlike an expectant father—the loom of impending responsibilities. He was the only son of aging parents with a predisposition for chronic illness. His father's mother had died of a stroke before her sixtieth birthday. His mother's sister had suffered with rheumatoid arthritis before experiencing the "women's troubles" that eventually led to her death. And diabetes stretched so far back in his father's lineage that Leon believed his ancestors died of the disease long before they had a name for it. More than once Victor had joked to friends that, when confronted with forms inquiring after family medical history, he simply checked the first four boxes without looking. (Though, the only reason Victor felt he could permit himself to make the joke was that he was thirty years old, earned $170,000 a year and knew that although he would not be able to spare his parents the misery of illness, he would at least be able to spare them the misery of illness compounded by the insult of poverty.)

After dinner Victor's mother, instead of saying goodbye at the doors of the elevator, insisted on walking Victor down to his car. Victor had not committed to going to Riga and she wanted him to understand—if he already did not—the effect his refusal would have on Leon. They both knew that Leon could be obsessive about the smallest things, and considering his condition, this was in some ways a blessing. As he sat at home alone every day, his obsessions kept his mind occupied. He could fashion his plans and make his phone calls. At the university library where Victor's mother worked, her co-workers all recognized Leon's voice. Before his retirement he'd rarely called, but now he no longer needed to ask for his wife by name.

"Of course you don't know this, but he calls me five or

six times a day. Over the last month all the time to consult about the preparations for the gravestone. You know how he is, he says he wants my advice. Should he send Sander all the money at once or half and half? Do I think he should make up a contract for Sander to sign or would Sander be offended? And then when they started talking about what kind of stone, what shape, what size. Finally, when it came time to compose an epitaph, he says to me, 'You studied literature.' There, at least, I think he actually listened to what I said."

Standing in the street beside his car, Victor explained again why the trip would be much more complicated than his father imagined. He had only two weeks for vacation. And it wasn't the kind of vacation where he would be in one place all the time. He would be visiting the only close friend he had retained from his time at Oxford. The previous year this friend had gotten married and Victor had been unable to attend the wedding. His friend wanted Victor to meet his wife and spend some time with them. They had been planning this trip for months. Not only had his friend coordinated his vacation to coincide with Victor's but so had his new wife. They had plans to travel through Scotland, Ireland and Wales. All the travel reservations had already been made. So, it wasn't that Victor didn't want to help put his father's mind at ease, but that there were other people involved and he could not change his plans without inconveniencing them.

"If you tell them why, they'll understand. People have emergencies."

"I know people have emergencies. But the grave has been there for twenty-five years. All of a sudden it's an emergency?"

"For your father it's an emergency."

"If he waits six months, I promise I'll book a ticket and go."

In his mother's deliberate pause, Victor heard what neither of them dared speak out loud. Leon was careful about his diet, monitored his blood sugar and took his insulin injections. There was nothing to say that he could not continue this way for twenty years. Nevertheless, Victor felt that it was irresponsible, even ominous, to project into the future—even six months—and presume that his father would still be there.

Meeting his mother's eyes, Victor knew that the decision had been made. And when his mother spoke it was no longer to convince him but rather to assure him that he was doing the right thing.

"I understand it will be unpleasant to disappoint your friends. But it's only three days. And, after all, this is your grandfather's and not some stranger's grave."

....

Late on a Saturday night Victor's flight made its approach to the Riga airport. On the descent Victor looked out his window at the flat, green Latvian landscape. His neighbour for the three-hour trip from Heathrow had been a garrulous, ruddy-faced Latvian in his seventies—a San Diego resident since 1947. Following the collapse of Communism, the man had returned to Latvia every summer for the fishing. When Victor informed him that he was undertaking his first trip to Latvia since his family's emigration in 1978, the man invited him to his cabin. Though the man was sincere and friendly, Victor couldn't help but hear his parents' refrain about innocent Latvians not retreating with the Nazis. Whether this was true or not, Victor was not exactly proud of the ease with which his mind slipped into clannish paranoia. But to maintain the necessary objectivity wasn't easy, particularly when buckled into an airplane full of blond heads.

In fact, after Los Angeles, and even London, Latvia struck him as remarkable in its blondness. At the customs desk, a pretty blond agent checked his passport. Tall blond baggage handlers handled the baggage. And it was a blond policewoman in a knee-length grey skirt who directed Victor up to the second floor where he could find a taxi. He had returned to the city of his birth, but no place had ever seemed less familiar. As he left the terminal, he even marvelled at the sky. His flight had landed after ten and he had spent close to an hour in the terminal, but when he stepped outside, the pavement, highway and outlying buildings were illuminated by some bright, sunless source.

At the curb a thin Russian hopped off the fender of a Volkswagen and reached for Victor's suitcase. He wore a New York Yankees T-shirt, Fila track pants and had the distinction of being not-blond. Identifying Victor immediately as a foreigner, he asked, "American?" Victor responded in Russian, speaking in a terser, gruffer register than he normally used—a register he hoped would help to disguise the extent of his foreignness, make him appear less dupable, less likely to be quoted an exorbitant fare. When the cab driver said, "Fifteen lats"—equivalent to twenty-plus American dollars—a price Victor still suspected was inflated, he growled his disapproval and, to his satisfaction, succeeded in having the fare reduced by one lat.

On the road to Jurmala, Victor—harbouring an appropriate level of resentment for the driver—rode in silence. He focused on the passing scenery. At that hour, nearly midnight, there were few other cars on the four-lane highway that led from the airport to Jurmala. The view was unspectacular. He registered certain banal observations. The road was smooth and clean. The passing cars were German, Swedish, Japanese—and clean. The few gas stations they passed appeared to be newly constructed. Victor kept expecting to feel something, to be somehow inspired. But all he could manage was: *I was born here, and I'm evaluating the infrastructure.*

The cab driver spoke over his shoulder and asked which hotel. Victor pronounced the name without turning his head.

"Villa Majori? Not bad. You know who owns it?"

"No."

"The former mayor of Jurmala."

Victor couldn't be sure, but it seemed the driver expected him to be impressed.

"He was mayor for six months. Now he has a hotel. The property alone is worth 250,000 lats."

"So, he's a crook."

"Of course he's a crook."

"Did you vote for him?"

"Did *I* vote for him? What difference does that make? Certain people decided he would be mayor, then later they decided he would no longer be mayor. It's not like that in America?"

"In America he'd have two hotels."

The driver laughed, inspiring in Victor a self-congratulatory and yet fraternal feeling.

"The mayor: a crook and a bastard, but I hear the hotel is good and that the girls he hires are very attractive."

Minutes later Victor discovered that the hotel was indeed modern, tidy and staffed—even at that late hour—by a pretty clerk. The hotel consisted of three floors, giving the impression that, before being converted to suit the needs of the former mayor, it had been someone's home. Victor found his room on the second floor and stood looking out the window at the flux of pedestrians on Jomas Street. The street was closed to all but pedestrian traffic and was flanked on either side by bars, restaurants and the odd hotel. Through his closed window he could hear the undifferentiated din of voices and music from rival bars. Had he wanted to sleep, the noise would have been infuriating, but though he'd hardly slept in two days, he felt exceedingly, even pathologically, alert.

So, as he watched the sky literally darken before his eyes—a change so fluid it felt as though he were watching time-lapse photography of dusk—Victor decided to call home.

As it was Saturday morning in Los Angeles, his mother picked up the phone. When she realized it was Victor, she deliberately kept her voice neutral so as not to attract Leon's attention.

"You're there?"

"I'm there."

"In the hotel?"

"In the hotel."

"On Jomas?"

"I can see it from my window."

"How does it look?"

"How did it look before?"

"People were strolling all day. Everyone dressed up. All year long girls thought only about getting a new dress for the summer."

Victor heard Leon's voice rising above his mother's, followed by the inevitable squabbling over the possession of the phone.

"You see, if I tell him who it is, he won't let me talk."

"What do you need to talk about? You can talk when he gets home. Has he spoken to Sander's son?"

Sander Rabinsky had a son in Riga whom Victor was supposed to contact upon his arrival in the city. Sander's son was named Ilya and happened, as Leon enthusiastically pointed out, also to be a lawyer. It had been Ilya who had informed Leon of Sander's death. After not hearing from Sander for several days, Leon had called repeatedly, left messages and kept calling until finally Ilya had answered the phone.

"Did you call him?"

"It's midnight."

"Call him first thing."

"I will."

"Good. So how is it over there?"

"Exactly like Los Angeles. Maybe better. The women are beautiful and there are no fat people."

"Latvians: they look good in uniforms and are wonderful at taking orders. God punished them with the Russians. The devil take them both. Don't forget to call Sander's son."

....

Victor slept only a few hours and awoke in spite of himself at first light. He lingered in bed, trying to will himself back to sleep, but after an hour of this futility, he rose, showered, dressed and ventured outside. He found Jomas Street deserted but for a handful of elderly city workers armed with straw brooms engaged in the removal of the evidence of the previous night's revelry. It was only five o'clock and Victor walked the length of Jomas Street, past the shuttered bars, small grocery stores and souvenir shops. The only place not closed at that hour was an Internet café attended by a teen-ager slumped behind the counter. Victor wrote a too-lengthy email to his friend in England. He had little new to say, having parted from his friend and his friend's wife less than a day before, but to kill time he reassured them that they should begin their trip without him and that he would join them as soon as he resolved the business with his grandfather's gravestone. At the very least, Victor joked, he would connect with them by the time they reached Dublin, where his friend's wife had promised to set him up with a former roommate. Victor knew little about the girl other than her name, Nathalie, and that in a picture from his friend's wedding she appeared as a slender, attractive, dark-haired girl in a bridesmaid's dress.

By eight o'clock Victor had eaten his complimentary breakfast in the hotel's dining room and decided, even though it was still possibly too early, to call Sander's son. He dialed from his room and a woman answered. Leon had told him that Ilya was married with a young son of his own. Speaking to the woman, Victor tried to explain who he was. He mentioned Sander's name, the gravestone and his father's name. Victor sensed a hint of displeasure in the way the woman replied, "Yes, I know who you are," but tried to dismiss it as cultural—Russians are not generally inclined to American-grade enthusiasm—and he was relieved when he heard no trace of the same tone in Ilya's voice.

"I spoke with your father. He said you would be coming," Ilya said.

Victor offered his condolences over Sander's death and

then accepted Ilya's invitation to stop at his apartment before proceeding to the cemetery.

Much as the travel agent had indicated, Victor found Dzintari station a few minutes' walk from his hotel. This route—Dzintari to Riga—was identical to the route he would have taken twenty-five years earlier in the summers when his parents rented a small cottage by the seashore. Somewhere, not far from his hotel, the cottage probably still existed, although Victor didn't expect that he could find it.

For the trip Victor assumed a window seat and watched as the train sped past the grassy banks of a river and then russet stands of skinny pines. Since it was a Sunday morning, and as he was heading away from the beach and in the direction of the city, there were few other people in his car. At the far end of the car were two young men with closely cropped hair sharing a quart of malt liquor, and several benches across from Victor, a grandmother was holding the hand of a seri-ous little boy dressed in shorts, red socks and brown leather sandals no self-respecting American child would have con-sented to wear. Now and again, Victor caught the boy's eyes as they examined him. The boy's interest appeared to be drawn particularly by the plastic bag Victor held in his lap: a large Robinsons-May bag in which Victor carried a bottle of tequila for Ilya and a small rubber LA Lakers basketball that he had purchased for Ilya's son.

From the train station Victor followed Ilya's directions and walked through the centre of the city. Ilya lived on Bruninieku

Street, formerly called Red Army Street, in the apartment Sander had occupied for over fifty years. It was there, on Red Army Street, that Sander and Leon had become acquainted. They had been classmates in the Number 22 Middle School. Leon had lived around the corner and spent many afternoons playing soccer in the very courtyard where Victor now found himself. The courtyard and the building were older than the fifty years, closer to eighty or ninety, and the dim stairwell leading to the second floor suggested the handiwork of some pre–World War II electrician.

Victor climbed stone steps, sooty and tread-worn to con-cavity, and squinted to read graffiti of indeterminate prove-nance. Some was in Latvian and seemed nationalistic in nature; some was in Russian and, if he read carefully, he could make out what it meant: "Igor was here." "Nadja likes cock." "Pushkin, Mayakovsky, Vysotsky."

Victor found the number of Ilya's apartment stencilled above the peephole and rang the buzzer. He heard a child's high and excited cry of "Papa," and then Ilya opened the door. He was slightly shorter than Victor but was of the same type—a type that in America could pass for Italian or Greek but that in Latvia wasn't likely to pass for anything other than itself. Ilya wore a pair of house slippers, track pants and a short-sleeved collared shirt. Standing at Ilya's side was a little blond girl, no older than five. The little girl seemed excited to see Victor.

"Papa, look, the man is here."

Ilya gently put a hand on her shoulder and edged her out of the doorway.

"All right, Brigusha, let the man inside."

Victor followed Ilya into the living room, where Ilya's wife was arranging cups, wafers and a small teapot on the coffee table. The mystery of genes and chromosomes accounted for the nearly identical resemblance between mother and daughter and, but for a fullness at the mouth, the complete absence of the father in the little girl's face.

As Victor, Ilya and the little girl entered the room, Ilya's wife straightened up, looked at Victor and appeared no happier at seeing him than she'd been at hearing his voice over the telephone. Ilya motioned for Victor to sit on the sofa and then performed the introductions.

"This is my wife, Salma, and Brigitta, our little girl."

Victor smiled awkwardly. He felt that he had made the mistake of taking his seat too soon. The upholstery claimed him in a way that made it difficult for him to lean forward or to rise. Undertaking the introductions while seated seemed wrong to the point of rudeness. As it was, he already felt less than welcome. He wanted to be on his feet, not only to shake hands but also to offer the gifts he had lugged in the Robinsons-May bag—though the prospect of getting to his feet immediately after sitting down and then presenting the inappropriate basketball to Ilya's daughter momentarily paralyzed him. He felt the temptation to explain the misunderstanding about the basketball but knew that to do so would be a betrayal of Leon; that it would conjure an image of his father as confused, inattentive, self-involved, possibly senile.

Doing his best to mask the exertion, Victor rose from the sofa and offered his hand to Salma and then, playfully, to the little girl. Because he knew that Salma didn't like him, Victor watched her face for some sign of détente, but as Brigitta's small hand gripped the tips of his fingers, Salma's smile merely devolved from token to weary. Her expression made Victor feel like a fraud even though, apart from trying to be social, he was quite sure he hadn't done anything fraudulent. Under different circumstances, Victor consoled himself, he wouldn't tolerate a woman like her.

Turning his attention from her, Victor reached into his bag, caring less now about the reaction to the basketball, and retrieved first the bottle of tequila and then the ball. To his relief, the little girl took the ball with genuine pleasure and bounced it on the stone floor with both hands.

Ilya, inspecting the bottle, looked up and watched as Brigitta chased the ball into the kitchen.

"Before she punctured it, she had a beach ball like that. She could bounce the thing all day. Brigusha, say thank you."

Victor, uncertain if he'd been commended or not, said that he hoped the gift was all right.

"You couldn't get her anything better. Right, Salma?"

Salma, for the first time, looked—though not quite happy—at least somewhat less austere.

"It's very nice. Thank you."

She then picked up the empty Robinsons-May bag that Victor had left on the floor.

"Do you need the bag back?"

"No."

"It's a good bag."

She called after her daughter.

"Brigusha, come here. Look at what a nice big bag the man left for you."

Carrying the ball, Brigitta returned to admire the bag.

"See what a big, fancy bag. You could keep all your toys in here. Come show the man how you can say thank you."

Brigitta looked up at Victor, down at her feet and then pressed her face into Salma's hip.

"Now you're shy?" Ilya said. "Maybe later you can show the man how you say thank you. She can say it in four languages. Russian, Latvian, German and English."

Placing the tequila on the table, Ilya asked his wife to bring glasses.

"Come, we'll sit. I should have put a bottle down to begin with."

Angling past the coffee table, Victor resumed his place on the sofa.

"What kind of alcohol is this?"

"Mexican. They make it from a plant that grows in the desert. It's very popular in America."

Salma returned with two glasses and Ilya poured.

"To new friendship," he proclaimed.

After Salma made the tea and distributed the wafers, she took Brigitta into a bedroom. From what Victor could see, that bedroom, plus another, along with a kitchen, bathroom and living room constituted the apartment. The ceilings were high, maybe twelve feet, and the floors and walls were in good repair. Also, the furniture, polished and solid, seemed to be many decades old and might have, for all Victor knew, qualified as antique.

"You like the apartment?" Ilya said.

"It would be hard to find one as good in Los Angeles."

"This apartment is the only home I've ever had. Now it's my inheritance. After the war my grandparents returned from the evacuation and moved here. My father grew up here, married here, and when I was born this is where he brought me from the hospital. As a boy I slept on this sofa, my parents in the smaller room, my grandparents in the larger. When my grandparents died, my parents took their room and I was given the smaller one. Now it's my turn to take the big bedroom and move Brigitta into the little one. You could say I've been waiting my entire life to move into the big room. Though, if you follow the pattern, you can see where I go from here."

"So don't move into the big room. Then maybe you'll live forever."

"Well, we haven't moved yet. Brigitta still calls it 'Grandfather's room.' She likes to go and see his white coat hanging on the hook."

"She's a good girl."

"Do you have children?"

"No."

"Married?"

"No."

"It's a different life in America."

"Probably not that different. At my age most Americans have children. Some are even married."

The mood had started to become a little too confessional for Victor's liking and he took it as a good sign when Ilya grinned.

"One day I'd like to visit America. Salma's English is very good. Until recently she even worked for an American software company. Owned by Russians from San Francisco, Jews, who left here, like you, in the 1970s. They returned to take advantage of the smart programmers and the cheap labour. But the company went bankrupt after the problems with the American stock market."

"Unfortunately, it's a familiar story."

" 'Capitalism,' as my father would have said. Though he wasn't much of a Communist. But when everyone was leaving, he wasn't interested. He liked it here. He was a doctor; he wanted to remain a doctor. He had no regrets. Not long ago, after your father contacted him, he said to me, 'You see. What if I'd left? I'd be collecting welfare in Brooklyn, and who would help blind Leon Shulman with his father's gravestone?' He had a real sense of humour."

. . . .

Wolf Shulman was buried at the "new" Jewish cemetery on Shmerle Street. An older cemetery, from before the war, could be found in the Moskovsky *farshtat*, a traditionally poor, working-class neighbourhood behind the train station. Before the Nazi occupation the neighbourhood had been predominantly Jewish and, during the Nazi occupation, it had served as the ghetto. Ilya said there wasn't much to see there but, if Victor liked, Ilya would show him around. The municipal courthouse, where Ilya worked as a prosecutor, was only a few minutes away by foot.

From Ilya's apartment Victor caught a bus that let out at the base of Shmerle Street. Shmerle, a winding tributary off the main road, rose to the cemetery and beyond. A concrete wall, painted a pale orange, encircled the cemetery. Victor followed the wall to the gates, where three old Russian women, wearing babushkas and wool socks, minded a wooden flower stall. Business appeared less than brisk, but as Victor neared the entrance, he saw a young couple select a bouquet of yellow carnations and so he did the same. He then passed through the gates and located the small stone building that served as the cemetery manager's office. Inside, the office was one single room, with dusty casement windows, a desk for the cemetery manager and a lectern upon which rested a thick, leather-bound book. Upon entering, Victor saw a short, heavy-set man wearing faded jeans, a pink cotton sweater and a black yarmulke examining a slip of paper that had been handed to him by the young couple with the yellow carnations. Victor heard the man ask, "*Berkovitz* or *Perkovitz*?" and the young woman reply, "Berkovitz. Shura Efimovna Berkovitz." "*Berko-vitz, Berkovitz,*" the man repeated, and shuffled to the lectern and opened the large book. "Year of death?" he inquired and, given the year, flipped pages and ran his finger down a column of handwritten names.

Once he found the name, the manager wrote down the section and row and pointed the young couple in the appro-priate direction. For his service, and for the upkeep of the cemetery, he drew their attention to a container for dona-tions. In a practised appeal that included Victor, the man said, "We have more dead than living. And the dead don't donate."

When the young couple left to seek Shura Berkovitz's grave, Victor introduced himself to the manager. For the sec-ond time that day, he was surprised to be so effortlessly rec-ognized. Using the same words Salma had used earlier that morning (though without the rancour), the manager said, "Yes, I know who you are."

Flipping more pages in the book, the manager looked for Wolf Shulman.

"Remind me, what year did he die?"

"1978."

"There. Shulman, Wolf Lazarovich," the manager said, and copied the information.

"And is everything ready for the new gravestone?"

"The grave is there. It's always ready. When the stonecutter brings the new stone, he'll also remove the old one. Very easy. Tik-tak."

"Is he here today?"

Ilya had told Victor that sometimes, particularly on Sundays, the stonecutter could be found at the cemetery. He also added that Victor would be well advised to speak to him as soon as possible because the stonecutter could be a difficult man to track down. Sander had expended no small amount of energy dealing with him.

"I'll call him at his shop," the cemetery manager said, and dialed the number.

Within seconds he was speaking to the stonecutter. He spoke partly in Yiddish and partly in Russian. After a very brief exchange, he hung up. Victor, trying to suppress his irritation, explained that he had wished to speak to the stonecutter himself.

"He said he can see you tomorrow morning. He's very busy right now, but he'll be able to speak to you then. He keeps an office at the Jewish Community Centre. He'll be waiting for you at 10:30."

"I understand. But, you see, I'm only here for a short time and I want to be sure there are no miscommunications."

"You shouldn't worry. I know of the matter. He knows of the matter. There will be no miscommunications. You'll see him tomorrow and everything will be just as you wish."

Victor paused, assumed an expression he often employed when dealing with obdurate lawyers and clients, an expression intended to imply sincere deliberation, and then said, "Nevertheless."

The cemetery manager raised his palms in a sign of surrender. He scribbled a number on a piece of paper.

"Here is the number. Please. I wouldn't want you to think I am interfering. I was only trying to help you. The stonecutter is one of those men who, when he is busy, doesn't like to be disturbed."

Victor took the number and dialed. After a short while he heard a man's terse hello. Before Victor could finish introducing himself, the man barked, "Tomorrow, 10:30," and hung up. Victor replaced the phone and turned reluctantly to face the cemetery manager's obsequious grin.

....

The cemetery at Shmerle had been hewn from a forest, but enough trees had been spared so as to retain a sense of the arboreal. Different types of trees—birch, elm, maple, ash—provided texture and shade and resembled in their randomness the different species of gravestones—marble, granite, limestone—that sprouted from the ground as naturally as trees. Other than being arranged in sections and rows, no other order had been imposed on the gravestones and so large dwarfed small, traditional opposed modern, and dark contrasted light. The only commonality between them was that each stone featured a photograph of the deceased and that in each photograph the deceased possessed the same grudging quality of expression. Soldiers, grandmothers, engineers, mathematicians: all stared into eternity with a face that declared not *I was alive*, but rather, *This was my life*. After walking some distance, Victor found his grandmother and grandfather wearing this same face.

Until he saw his grandmother's grave, Victor had at some level forgotten about it. That he carried only one bouquet reminded him of the extent to which he had forgotten. His grandmother had died when he was still an infant and so he had no memory of her at all. Somewhere there was a picture of the two of them together: a baby in the arms of a stout, prematurely old woman. Her gravestone confirmed what little he knew of her. "Etel Solomonovna Shulman, beloved wife, mother and grandmother. Died before her sixtieth birthday." This information, along with her photo, was etched onto a thick, rectangular slab of black granite. And this slab, almost three feet high, towered over a limestone monument one-third its size, already weather-worn and tilting slightly backwards. Seeing the two gravestones side by side, and having seen the other stones in the cemetery, Victor could understand his father's anguish. What was left for Wolf Shulman appeared insufficient and unjust. It seemed a slight against a man whose solemn face—due to the backwards tilting of the stone—appealed vaguely heavenwards with an expression that could also be interpreted as: *Is this all I deserve?*

After taking some pains to divide his bouquet into two equal halves, Victor paused and contemplated his grandparents' graves. The graves evoked in him a peculiar timbre of grief—grief over not what he had lost but over what he had never had. A baser, more selfish form of grief. The kind that only permitted him to mumble a self-conscious goodbye before turning back up the path. He then retraced his steps through the cemetery, stopping at times to appraise certain grave-stones, look at pictures and read names and dates. There were other members of his family buried here, and he discov-ered the grave of a great-uncle as well as some other graves with the last name Shulman—although he couldn't be sure if they were definitively his relations. The only other name he recognized appeared in a section occupied by more recent graves. On a reddish marble stone, he read the name Rabin-sky and saw a picture of a woman who could only have been Ilya's mother. The picture, like all such pictures, was not of the best quality, but Victor could discern enough to draw the obvious conclusion. And beside this grave was another, still lacking a stone, but with a small plastic sign pressed into the soft earth on which was stencilled the name S. Rabinsky.

It was only noon when Victor left the cemetery and, though he felt the sluggishness of three days without sleep, he decided to take a tour of the city. He caught a bus back into the vicinity of Ilya's apartment and then walked to the heart of medieval Riga. The city had been established in the twelfth century and had, throughout its history, been the subject of every Baltic power. Poles and Swedes had tramped through its cobblestone streets. In the twentieth century alone—but

for a brief spell of interwar independence—it had belonged
to the Tsar, the Kaiser, Stalin, Hitler and then Stalin once
more. But although it had been repeatedly contested over
two world wars, it had never been the site of any major battle. Occupiers marched in, retreated, were replaced by other
occupiers who then retreated, firing a few parting shots but
effecting little damage. And so Victor was able to observe
the baroque architecture, pass through winding alleyways
and visit the Domsky Cathedral, home to a world-famous
organ. Later, by leaving the old city, he was also able to find
many examples of art nouveau buildings, with their elabo-
rate stucco figures and faces. However, not being particularly interested in architecture, Victor saw just enough to
get a sense of the place. And after he'd acquired this sense,
he took a seat at an outdoor café and ate his lunch in view
of pedestrians, vendors, drunks, policemen and bus drivers.
In its constituent parts the city displayed itself and seemed,
with its imported cars and Western fashions, none the worse
for fifty years of Soviet rule.

On the drive back to Jurmala, Victor allowed himself to
drift off. It was the deepest sleep he had experienced since
leaving Los Angeles and, when his cab reached the hotel, a
tremendous effort was required for him to rouse himself. He
wanted nothing other than to sleep until morning, but back
at the front desk, there were messages waiting for him from
his father and from Ilya. So, tired as he was, Victor began
by calling Ilya and recounting the episode at the cemetery

manager's office. The incident, according to Ilya, was consistent with the man's character.

"But you have to consider how many others are practising his trade. The man has no competition and so, unfortunately, he's become arrogant."

Ilya wished Victor luck and then invited him to come to the courthouse after his meeting with the stonecutter. He framed the invitation in collegial terms. As a fellow jurist, Ilya imagined that Victor possessed some professional curiosity.

"This way," Ilya said, "you will be able to see the fabulous workings of the Latvian legal system."

Victor then placed his call home. This time Leon answered, after hardly a single ring, as though he had been sitting, primed, by the telephone. Whatever reservations Victor harboured about the cemetery manager and stonecutter, he knew better than to reveal them to his father. To Leon's detailed questions, he responded honestly but without elaboration. Yes, he had gone and seen Sander's son. Yes, he had been received cordially. Yes, he had given the *child* the present and the *child* had been pleased. Yes, he had been to the cemetery, seen his grandparents' graves and left flowers. And yes, he had also spoken with the cemetery manager and with the stonecutter—the latter of whom he had not seen personally but would the very next morning.

After the conversations with his father and with Ilya, Victor discovered—to his frustration—that he had lost his overwhelming need for sleep. However, the prospect of another sleepless night was unbearable, and so Victor drew the blinds, climbed into bed and resolved to nurture even the slightest vestige of fatigue. It was still quite early, a little after six o'clock, and he thought that if only he could fall asleep, he would be able to remain blissfully unconscious until his wake-up call at seven the next morning. But once again, like the previous night, his body refused to co-operate. He slept only fitfully, waking up disoriented, sometimes because of voices in the street, other times because of some malformed thought. At one point he found himself bolt upright, unsure whether or not he had indeed requested a wake-up call. He then spent what felt like an eternity torn over whether or not to call the front desk and confirm yes or no. Later, he lost the better part of an hour recreating the scene at the cemetery manager's office and formulating alternate scenarios in which he didn't come off looking like an idiot. Eventually, in despair, he turned on the television and watched an American action movie dubbed in Latvian with Russian subtitles.

At five in the morning, Victor was back among the sweepers on Jomas Street. The sky was cloudless and approaching full daylight. Victor made a circuit of Jomas, covering its entire length, and then turned north and walked the few blocks to the beach, which, like the streets, was largely deserted. Narrow and white, it stretched from east to west, seemingly to infinity. The tide was still high and sandpipers skittered neurotically at the fringes of the waves. A short distance up the beach from him, two middle-aged women in bathing suits were balancing against each other and advancing gingerly out into the Baltic. They had already progressed about fifty yards but the water was not yet to their waists. The sight triggered Victor's first memory of his Soviet childhood: stepping out into a dark-blue sea, conscious of danger but feeling as though he could go a great distance before he had anything to fear.

....

To find the Jewish Community Centre, Victor crossed a large municipal park and looked for the spire of a Russian Orthodox church. As he was extremely early, he trolled past the community centre, made sure he was in the right place, and then sat and waited in the park until he thought it was reasonable to go and look for the stonecutter.

The community centre, contrary to Victor's expectations, was a substantial building—four storeys tall and designed in the art nouveau style. Though it had a fairly dark and dreary-looking lobby, a broad stone stairway led to the upper floors, all of which benefited from an abundance of natural light. Not knowing whom to ask or where to look, Victor climbed the staircase and roamed the hallways, hoping to stumble upon something that would announce itself as the stonecutter's office. He wandered for what seemed like a long time, finding no explicit sign of the stonecutter— though, instead, he found an adult choir practising Hebrew songs in a rehearsal room, a grand theatre with crumbling plaster and a seating capacity of hundreds, the locked doors of "The Latvian Jewish Museum," and a tribute dedicated to a handful of Latvians who had protected Jews during the war. He found these things, but he found little in the way of assistance until a young Latvian woman emerged from an office and cheerily informed Victor that the stonecutter did indeed use a room in the building but that he kept no regular hours and she hadn't seen him that morning. However, keen to help, she led Victor down one floor and pointed out the stonecutter's door. She even knocked, waited and then apologized profusely, as if she were personally responsible for the stonecutter's absence. There was a phone in her office, she said, if Victor wanted to call the stonecutter, and also magazines, if he felt the need to occupy himself while waiting.

Seeing no other recourse, Victor followed the woman to her office and made the pointless phone call. The stonecutter was admittedly only fifteen minutes late, and the fact that he did not pick up the phone could actually be construed as a good sign—the man was on his way—so there was, in essence, no logical reason for despair. And yet, each unanswered ring reinforced Victor's suspicion that the man was simply not going to show up. The stonecutter wasn't going to show up and Victor would nevertheless have to wait for him. What choice did he have? He would wait an hour, maybe an hour and a half, and make intermittent phone calls to the stonecutter. And then, when the man still refused to appear, Victor would trudge to the municipal courthouse and suffer through some insipid Latvian hearing and then appeal to Ilya like a helpless child.

Victor put down the phone. Beside him, the woman looked on with a doleful expression, and Victor dreaded that, at any moment, she was going to repeat her offer of the telephone and the magazines. He couldn't recall if he'd seen a pay-phone down in the lobby, but he was quite sure that he had seen one at the park. Calling from the park would require that he go somewhere and make change, and then walk the two blocks from the community centre to the park every time he wanted to make a phone call—thereby introducing a risk of missing the stonecutter in the event that the man made a brief appearance at his office—but all this still seemed pref-erable to remaining, for even one second longer, the object of this woman's sympathy.

Once again, Victor walked up and down the staircase. He listened to the choir and then descended to the lobby, where he found a handful of elderly Jews convened at a table, speak-ing Yiddish, chewing sandwiches and playing cards. Victor stood for a few moments debating whether or not to go out-side until a man brushed past him, hunched, bent under the weight of some psychological burden. He wore an ancient raincoat, a beaten fedora and carried a briefcase. The man made his way for the doors of the public toilet and Victor heard him muttering to himself: "If only to go and shit like a human being."

Victor decided to go outside.

Sitting in the park—having run the same coin through the payphone for the third time—it struck Victor as funny that there had been a time when the purpose of his vacation had had absolutely nothing to do with Latvia. That at some point he had conceived of a relaxing trip with friends, touring parts of the UK he had been unable to see as an exchange student. And, when the idea of the trip to Riga had been introduced (or, rather, imposed), he had treated it only as a minor deviation. A filial duty quickly and easily dispatched. But now, feeling slightly delirious with exhaustion—but also too nervous and preoccupied to be able to sleep—he felt it was inconceivable that he would ever reunite with his friend and see Ireland, Scotland and Wales. Such a trip was a dream, a ridiculous joke. Totally unavailable to him because his fate was to be perpetually trapped in Latvia pursuing a stonecutter, thinking obsessively about gravestones. In short, becoming his father.

Victor laughed out loud like a lunatic. It was possible that people at neighbouring benches turned and stared. He didn't bother to check one way or the other. He had made his phone calls; he had knocked on the stonecutter's door; he had sat and waited. It was now time to go and walk to the courthouse and continue the farce. He rose, crossed the park, and in a matter of minutes he had passed the train station, entered the courthouse, submitted to a metal detector and gone off in search of Ilya. He didn't need to look very long. Unlike the Jewish Community Centre, the courthouse possessed an information window at which Victor was able to learn the number of Ilya's courtroom. And, for what felt like the first time on his trip, he arrived somewhere at precisely the right moment. As he turned down the hallway, he saw two policemen escorting a handcuffed defendant into the courtroom followed by a small group of spectators: a young woman, a teenage boy and an older woman—presumably the defendant's family. Victor attached himself to the end of the procession and found a seat inside the small courtroom.

As opposed to most of the buildings Victor had seen in Riga, the courthouse was new and therefore outfitted with most of the contemporary trappings. The doors locked automatically when a session was in order, there was the faint cooling whir of air conditioning, and all of the courtroom furniture—though constructed from Latvian pine—had a vague Ikea-like quality. At the very back of the courtroom, to the right of the door, the accused sat on a bench inside a little gated prisoner's dock. Along the wall, just ahead of him, the two policemen sat on their benches. They were both young men, in green uniforms, barely in their twenties but already possessing the dull, indolent posture common to all court officers. Victor had his place across the aisle from the policemen. Behind him were the younger woman and the teenage boy and ahead of him was the old woman.

When Victor had entered the courtroom, there was no sight of the bailiff, judge or—more to the point—Ilya. Only the defence attorney, a tall, thin woman with tired, hound-like features, was present. Ilya did not appear until the bailiff emerged from the back door and called the session to order. All were made to rise while the judge mounted his podium. He was dressed in a burgundy robe and wore a chain of ornamental, golden medallions—evidently some folkloric symbol of Latvian authority. After the judge assumed his position, there followed the routine sequence of statements and exchanges—all of them in Latvian.

Victor understood hardly anything that happened over the next hour. He had no idea what the man had done to warrant his confinement, and he couldn't determine the purpose of the proceedings. He assumed they were preliminary, since, at one point, the defendant made a plea of not guilty. However, beyond that, the sense of things was impenetrable. And so, Victor paid attention only long enough to register that Ilya, in his suit and tie, seemed to be a good lawyer. He was organized, spoke succinctly and carried himself with an aloofness that bordered on menace. All of which probably didn't bode well for the man in handcuffs, who sat in the prisoner's dock looking not so much like a criminal but rather like a weary commuter waiting for the train. Victor assumed the same attitude of forbearance from the woman and the teenage boy as he heard not a sound behind him. The only person showing any sign of distress was the old woman in the front row. She had been in tears from the outset of the proceedings and, as time wore on, her breathing became shallower and more laboured. Though the air conditioning worked fine, Victor saw perspiration in the folds of her neck. She drank water from a plastic, teddy bear–shaped bottle—a kind manufactured to contain honey—and alternately wiped her eyes with a handkerchief and attempted to cool herself with a paper fan. But all to little effect, as, ultimately, her breathing seized up and Victor was convinced that she was on the verge of a heart attack. It was only at this point that the judge turned his attention to her and considered a pause in the proceedings, but, when she managed to collect herself, things resumed as before.

The hearing was the last of the day for Ilya, and so, at its conclusion, he suggested that they go and have lunch. They stopped at a small cafeteria, where Victor bought half a dozen meat and cabbage buns and two bottles of Latvian beer. They then walked back to the municipal park where Victor had already spent much of his morning. On the way Ilya explained what had transpired in the courtroom.

It was, as Victor had surmised, an arraignment. The man had already spent six months in custody waiting for the date. He would probably wait another several months before his next appearance. His crime was serious though not uncommon. He was charged with attempting to murder his boss. The man was a mechanic and had worked in an auto shop. He had been on the job for three months—the standard probationary period during which a new employee is paid poorly, if at all. After three months the boss is legally bound to either keep him on full-time or let him go. Generally, to avoid the higher taxes associated with having full-time employees, a boss will let the person go and find another—there being no shortage of people, desperate and willing to work for three months in the hopes that an employer might keep them on. In this case, the man claimed that his boss had promised to keep him. But when he came to work after his probationary period, he found someone else at his post. His boss told him to go to hell and so he stabbed him in the neck with a screwdriver.

Ilya assumed that the boss probably had it coming, but he had no choice but to prosecute. If he didn't, then every boss would be walking around with a screwdriver in his neck.

"So what will he get for stabbing his boss in the neck?"

"Hard to say. Ten years? Or nothing. He'll say it was self-defence. The boss attacked him. He supports a wife, a younger brother. Nobody really wants to put him in jail. But who knows? Maybe things will turn out badly and he'll be put away for a long time."

"Which will probably be the end of the old woman."

Ilya considered this and then confessed that he had his doubts about the old woman. It struck him as peculiar that while the rest of the family sat in the back, she had taken her place in the front. Obviously, the old woman was supposed to be the defendant's mother, but this wasn't something anyone had bothered to verify. So she could just as well have been any old woman off the street. Which meant that there was nothing to say that the family hadn't scraped three lats together and paid her to come to the courthouse and act hysterically. Such things were not without precedent. Though, for an arraignment, Ilya believed, it was a waste of money. But one couldn't blame the old woman. She probably received sixty lats a month as a pension, equivalent to $150. And, Ilya said, he didn't need to describe to Victor what it was like to live on $150 a month.

They entered the park and Ilya sought out a vacant bench in the shade. It was now early afternoon and much quieter than when Victor had been there in the morning. There were a few young mothers with children and strollers. Now and again, a businessman strode past speaking into a cellphone. A few tourists stopped to buy ice cream and study their maps. Victor sipped his beer and wondered if he should admit to Ilya that he had absolutely no idea what it meant to live on $150 a month in Riga. Judging from Ilya's tone, he gathered that $150 a month was a pathetic sum. It certainly didn't sound like a lot of money, but, then again, Latvia wasn't Los Angeles and, had Ilya phrased things differently, Victor could just as easily have been convinced that, in Latvian terms, $150 was a fortune. And though Victor subscribed to a sober view of the world and of the forces that ruled it—forces for whom the financial welfare of old ladies was generally not a top priority—he was in a strange country and therefore prone to a higher level of credulity; liable, practically, to believe the opposite of everything he believed.

"Do you want to know how much money I make?" Ilya said.

Then he answered his own question before Victor had a chance to object.

"Two hundred lats a month. This is considered a good salary. Just enough so that I will think twice before taking a bribe. My father made the same as a dermatologist with forty years' experience. Salma, when she worked for the Americans, made 250 lats. For a time, with three salaries, a total of 650 lats a month, we were relatively well off."

Ilya then proceeded to quote a litany of expenses, most of which, he said, were common to everyone in the city. Rent, food, transportation, miscellaneous items for children and the elderly. The figure he quoted for rent alone exhausted the total of the old woman's pension. There was, Ilya said, really no such thing as disposable income. This was why, to cite an extreme example, most of Riga's prostitutes had abandoned the city for points west. (And as for an explanation of the young mothers in the park, the businessmen, the pretty girls in summer dresses—in short, the reason Victor saw no squalor—well, it was Europe, after all. Not Africa. One good suit, one designer blouse—though second-hand from Germany—represented the difference between self-respect and despondency.)

Ilya recited all of this information with detachment, as though he were addressing something merely statistical, academic, impersonal. His voice contained no resentment, which was why, when he asked Victor how much money he made, Victor felt less than his normal reticence to respond.

However, he chopped fifty thousand off the number, which, given the context, still sounded obscenely excessive.

"But," Victor qualified, "I work for a large firm. We do most of our business with corporations. Someone doing your job would make less. And then you still have to adjust for the higher cost of living . . ."

He realized that his was not a very persuasive argument. It was, even in terms of Los Angeles, not a very persuasive argument. He made a lot of money. Probably more than he deserved. But, then again, he knew of others who earned even more and deserved even less. (Though he didn't expect that this was a rationalization Ilya would likely appreciate.)

Ilya leaned back on the bench and regarded, as though with intense botanical interest, the leaves and branches of the shade tree.

"I have some money saved up. Enough to send Salma and Brigitta to America. As I say, Salma is an accomplished programmer and her English is very good. And Brigitta is young and will easily learn the language. I am the only impediment. But I have my job here and am prepared to wait until they are ready for me."

Ilya then turned his attention from the tree and focused on Victor. As Ilya prepared to speak, Victor noted an inchoate defensiveness in the set of his features, as though Ilya, like a teenage suitor, was poised for imminent rejection; prepared, at any moment, to dismiss the proposition with "never mind." Which was precisely what he said, but not before he said:

"I'm not asking for money." And not before Victor replied: "I do not practise that kind of law."

"But perhaps someone in your firm?"

"We deal only with corporations. Trade issues. Never individual immigration cases."

Which—other than the exceptions made for the sons, nephews and mistresses of wealthy clients—was the truth. Immigration cases were frustrating and time-consuming. Victor had not personally been involved in any, but he knew that they entailed a morass of paperwork and almost always ended in recriminations. He couldn't in good conscience agree to undertake any such thing. Given the choice, he would have actually preferred it if Ilya had asked for money.

"And what about other means?"

"What other means?"

"Marriage."

"But you are already married."

"We could divorce. Temporarily, of course. I have heard it done."

"And then what?"

"Salma could marry an American."

"Just like that?"

"How else?"

"And where would she find this American?"

Which, immediately, Victor understood was a stupid question.

"Never mind," Ilya said. "I see that it is asking too much."

Victor considered explaining, so far as he knew, the problems inherent even in this option, to try and exonerate himself, to impress upon Ilya the impracticality, and, beyond that, he considered lying, consenting to fill out forms, marry the man's wife, adopt his daughter, do whatever (since it was pitifully clear that between him and the stonecutter remained—even if only tenuously—Ilya), but he couldn't quite bring himself to do it. Instead, he sat beside Ilya and resigned himself to a punitive silence.

After some time, as if having reached a conclusion, Ilya repeated, "Never mind," and ended the silence.

"I realize that this isn't why you came here," Ilya said.

With each word he distanced himself from the man who had, only moments before, offered Victor his wife and child.

"Fortunately, your problem is easier to solve. I will call the stonecutter for you."

Ilya rose and went to the phone booth even though Victor was sure that he hadn't said anything to him about his most recent frustrations. And when Victor approached the phone booth, Ilya was already dialing a number. Then, in a matter of moments, he was speaking in Latvian, exhibiting the same bloodless composure he had evinced in the courtroom. The conversation did not last very long and Ilya did most of the talking. Once again, as at the cemetery manager's office, Victor felt himself excluded from considerations related to his own life. His input wasn't requested except to establish the departure time of his flight the next day.

When the conversation was over, Ilya exited the phone booth. "If you like, he can see us now," he announced.

"That was the stonecutter?"

"Yes."

"Is he at the community centre?"

"No."

"So, where is he?"

"At his shop. In the Moskovsky *farshtat*. It's possible to walk, although I would recommend a cab. A cab would get us there in ten minutes. We can get one easily on Brivibas Street."

Ilya half-turned in the direction of the street, ready to hail the cab, as if Victor's consent was foregone and incidental.

Angered by Ilya's presumptuousness, and momentarily unsure of what he wanted, Victor said, "What if I don't want to go?"

"You don't want to go?"

"I don't understand the rush."

"I thought you leave tomorrow."

"In the afternoon. I could see him in the morning."

"But he can see you now."

"I waited for him for two hours today. Where was he then?"

Victor saw that Ilya regarded him as one might a child or a dog, as some thing ruled by impulse and deficient in reason.

"I couldn't say. Though I imagine if we went you could ask him yourself."

The flatness of Ilya's tone discouraged Victor from asking anything further. Which was fine, since Victor no longer had anything to ask. He now recognized that he was in a situation that provided for only a binary choice. He could go with Ilya and see things through to their conclusion—whatever that might be—or he could refuse and claim the transitory pleasure of refusal. Those were his choices. There was nothing else. Calling the stonecutter and repeating his mistake at the cemetery was out of the question. And though he had misgivings about the likelihood of things turning out right, he also had an almost inexorable curiosity to finally meet the stonecutter. It seemed ridiculous—and likely a symptom of sleep deprivation and delirium—but he had begun to doubt the very fact of the stonecutter's existence. And he entertained the thought—in some sub-rational recess—that meeting the stonecutter might be like meeting God or the President or the Wizard of Oz. Equal parts disappointment and reward, but that, at least, the truth would be revealed.

....

Victor followed Ilya out to Brivibas Street, where, as predicted, they had no trouble finding a cab. Ilya rode up front and directed the driver while Victor sat in the back seat. The driver navigated along streets now familiar to Victor. They passed through the medieval city, looped behind the central markets and train station, and followed a route that brought them to the courthouse and the limit of Victor's knowledge. They then continued beyond the courthouse, south, into what generically could have been described as the "bad part of town." The change was abrupt, as though the result of a civic consensus: no tourists expected beyond this point. The streets were grey and dingy. Old buildings deteriorated unchecked. Not infrequently, Victor saw listing, wooden hovels—seemingly anomalous in an urban setting—beside concrete apartment houses. People moved about the streets, tending to their everyday affairs, but there were also shadowy figures loitering in the doorways. In America, the place would have qualified as a slum, depressing and interesting only in a sordid way. Here it was different only because it was old. It had been a slum for generations. Nazis had commanded here and perpetrated horrific crimes. All of this invested a sense of historical gravity, which made the slum feel like more than just a slum. And, assuming he didn't get mugged or clubbed to death, Victor thought it fitting that he should come here to get to the bottom of things.

After driving for several more minutes, Ilya pointed to a dark-green cottage and instructed the driver to stop. Victor then paid the driver and joined Ilya at the cottage's entrance. They stood there for a short while, but Ilya offered nothing in the way of explanation, not even a word to assure Victor that the dilapidated structure—bearing nothing to identify it as the stonecutter's shop or as a place of business of any kind—was where they needed to be. Victor had expected to find heavy machinery and stacked rock, but there was only a peeling facade, drawn curtains, uncut grass, and a dirt path that turned ninety degrees at the front steps and wound around the side of the house. Taking this path, Ilya led Victor the length of the house and into a yard dominated by a Mitsubishi pickup truck with a sunken rear suspension. The truck had been backed into the yard so that its tailgate was only a few feet from the doors of a garage and from a large manual winch. The winch looked ancient, a relic from previous centuries, but Victor could see that it was still very much in use. By its heavy rope, it suspended a rough marble obelisk three feet in the air. The obelisk spun lazily, as though it had only recently been disturbed.

Ilya placed a hand on the obelisk, indicated the garage and said, "Well, here you have him."

Victor stepped past a door and looked into the garage. Looking back at him was a man in his sixties. He wore scuffed work pants, a sleeveless undershirt, and he had the hands and arms befitting a man who spent his days working with stone. He sat on a low stool with his legs splayed out before him. In one hand he held an abrasive cloth that he had been using to polish a granite tombstone propped up against a nearby wall. He blinked sullenly and looked very much like someone who hadn't been happy to see anyone in years.

"Shimon," Ilya said, "I brought you your client."

Shimon blinked again and showed no indication that he had heard what Ilya said.

Ilya gave the obelisk a firm shove, putting the weight in motion and eliciting squeals of protest from the winch.

"Aren't you even going to say thank you, you old goat?"

"Go to the devil," Shimon said, "and take him with you."

"You shouldn't talk like that. He came all the way from America just to see you."

"All the worse for him."

Shimon glared from Victor to Ilya as though trying to determine which of them he despised more. For a moment Victor wondered if maybe the old man didn't have him confused with someone else. He'd not yet said one word to the stonecutter—barely looked at him, done nothing more than show up—and yet the man seemed to loathe him in a personal way. Victor found it unsettling, like the opprobrium of a cripple or a religious person. However, it didn't appear to bother Ilya, who responded to the stonecutter's hatred with a patrician smugness.

"Listen, if you don't want the business, we'll leave."

Shimon shrugged, hatred undiminished, but he was evidently not prepared to lose the business. Though, what business, Victor could not quite figure out. Seeing as how the money had been sent months ago and the work reportedly done.

Shimon lifted his face to Victor.

"Well, did you come from America to stand here like a mute? What is it you want from me?"

It could only be, Victor thought, that the man had confused him with someone else. Either that or he suffered from a mental illness.

"I spoke to you yesterday. We had an appointment for this

morning. I waited for you for hours. We were supposed to discuss the gravestone for my grandfather's grave. Work which I was told you had finished. Work for which you have already been paid. So, how exactly do you mean what do I want?"

"Who told you it was finished?"

"His father promised my father it would be finished. Money was wired. Are you saying it's not finished?"

"Ask your friend the parasite if it's finished."

Shimon jerked his head toward Ilya, the parasite, who had allowed a shadow to fall over his smugness.

"You see how he talks. You see what it's like to deal with him. My father literally spent weeks trying to have a reasonable conversation with him. And though I saw the trouble he was having, my father refused to let me intervene. Now, you've seen the Latvian legal system. You have seen where I work. It's nothing to be proud of. But, for what it's worth, it gives me access to certain people. And, if absolutely necessary, I can complicate someone's life." Ilya frowned in the stonecutter's direction. "Not that it's something I enjoy. What's to enjoy? Old men like him pass through the court every day. You'd have to be a sick person to enjoy making someone's miserable life even more miserable. Right?"

Ilya smiled philosophically at Victor, his eyes seeking confirmation, as though the question had not been rhetorical.

Just to be clear, he repeated it. "Right?"

"Right."

"But what choice do I have with someone like him?"

From the roof of his skull, Victor felt the spreading of a vaporous warmth. It filled him, like helium but not exactly, making him feel as though he were very light and very heavy all at once. It took him a second to identify this sensation as a powerful swell of fatigue. His legs felt like pillars, rooted into the ground, and yet he believed he might tip over.

Out of the corner of his eye, he thought he saw a lumbering, slow-witted man. The man was Shimon's son. He helped his father load and unload the heavy rocks. Victor turned to get a better look, but when he did he saw only Shimon sitting by himself in the garage. Victor turned back to Ilya.

"What does any of this have to do with my grandfather's gravestone?"

Ilya wavered before him. For a second blurry and then immaculately sharp.

"Let me explain it to you," Ilya said. "Three weeks ago my father got on a bus to go and see this man. This man who could not be relied upon to keep an appointment or return a phone call. On a hot day, after working for eight hours, at five o'clock, when the buses are full, my father had to ride across town. Before he got here he had a heart attack. They had to stop the bus. We only received a phone call when he was already in the hospital. I, my daughter, my wife, none of us even had a chance to say goodbye. This is what it has to do with your grandfather's gravestone. My father, who from the goodness of his heart agreed to help. My father, whom your father only pestered. Calling all the time. And then wanting to negotiate payment in installments. As if my father was a thief. And later sent him a *contract*."

Ilya spat the word *contract* out as if a more offensive word did not exist in the Russian language.

"This is what it has to do with anything. That my father killed himself over this gravestone. This gravestone that nobody would ever even visit. And what did my father get in return? Never a thank you. Only a hundred lats for his trouble. A hundred lats that won't even buy a stone a fifth as big for his memory. Now you tell me if that's fair."

Through the murk of fatigue, Victor heard the things Ilya said, but his brain processed only the rudiments: my father, your father, my father, your father. If there was an argument here, Victor didn't see how anyone could hope to win it. There was nothing to win. There was Sander, an old man suffering a heart attack on a cramped city bus: Ilya's father, but an abstraction to Victor. And there was Leon, an abstraction to Ilya, but as real to Victor as if he were standing before him. There he was, stumbling around the apartment, feeling the walls. There he was, every morning, in his track suit, doing deep knee bends and other ludicrous Soviet calisthenics. There he was, injecting himself with insulin and fretting about one thing or another at the kitchen table. His father.

"I thought I would give you a chance. If you would help," Ilya said. "And even now, I give you a chance. You can buy yourself another gravestone. God knows you have the money.

Give this old bastard the business he doesn't deserve. And I'll send you a photo to prove it gets done."

In a daze, Victor didn't even quite remember refusing the arrangement. Because he was already picturing his cab ride and the blur of pine trees on the way to Jurmala. And he was already in his hotel room, lying in bed, asleep and having a dream in which Nathalie, the Irish bridesmaid, appeared to him either on the beach in Jurmala or on the beach in Los Angeles—maybe both—and in which she professed her undying love, had sex with him, became his wife and then—with the confounding logic of dreams—transformed into Salma, who, stranger still, did nothing to undermine the benign quality of the dream but rather, in some illicit way (like the wrongest dream involving a relative), only enhanced the sense of pleasure. And then he awoke and dialed and had a conversation with Leon. A conversation in which Leon asked him how everything went. If he met the stonecutter. If he saw the gravestone. If everything looked as it should. And he answered his father, saying yes about the stonecutter, yes about the gravestone. Yes about everything. He answered him and said that everything was perfect, just the way he imagined it.

The Russian Riviera

"SOME BUSINESSMEN" WAS HOW Skinny Zyama had described the two gangsters from New Jersey.

"You want me there for a meeting with businessmen?" Kostya had asked.

"You have other plans on a Wednesday afternoon?"

"No."

"Wear a jacket," Zyama had said.

Now, stationed as instructed beside Skinny Zyama's mahogany desk, Kostya appraised the gangsters. Zyama had placed two leather armchairs in front of his desk, but only the smaller of the two had consented to sit. The larger one, the one doing all of the talking, had turned his chair sideways and perched himself on its arm. Instinctively, Kostya gauged both men's weights. They were both wearing suits, but that made no difference. Kostya had proven many times that he could guess a man's weight within one kilo even if he was dressed in heavy winter clothing. It was one of Kostya's few demonstrable skills, which—like his other skills—had brought him little profit. In Siberia, his father would occasionally take him to the bar to amuse his friends and to wager a bottle of vodka with skeptical strangers.

Conditioned by years at the gym, Kostya's mind conjured a man's weight and class, just as, seeing an apple, it conjured taste and smell. He'd barely considered the gangsters before his mind had announced: sixty-four kilos and eighty-five kilos— welterweight and cruiserweight. The larger gangster looked powerful through the back and shoulders, but he carried himself arrogantly, gestured excessively with his hands and punctuated his demands by thrusting out his chin. In contrast, the smaller one moved hardly at all. He kept his hands folded in his lap and followed the conversation with his eyes. His neck and his ankles were thin, and he was pale in the manner of someone who is either very sick or very spartan. Of the two, Kostya supposed the smaller man posed the greater danger, though, to be precise, the greatest danger was posed by neither of them. The greatest danger was posed by Skinny Zyama, who had assumed an obnoxious air of invulnerability.

"These are competitive times. You could benefit from our help," the larger gangster said.

"The place is busy four nights a week. Impossible to get a table Friday or Saturday without a reservation. We have the best Vegas-style floor show in the city. Professional dancers trained in Russia. Where's my competition?" Zyama asked.

"There are other restaurants. They could become more successful."

"The other restaurants are run by imbeciles. Their customers are people who couldn't get a table here."

"With the right guidance those restaurants could improve. With connections they could attract popular entertainers from New York and New Jersey."

"Listen, Alla Pugacheva and Arkady Raikin could perform every Saturday night for a month and those idiots would still find a way to lose money."

"There are also other possibilities. Something unfortunate could happen to your restaurant or to you."

Zyama, who had been reclining in his suede captain's chair, tilted forward and made a production of looking the gangster in the eye. "You think you're the first ones to come in here? Understand: I'm in business all these years not because I give money to every hoodlum with his hand out."

Kostya watched the larger gangster unbutton his jacket and slide his hand inside. Cursing Skinny Zyama, Kostya took a step in the gangster's direction. If the man had a gun, there wasn't much he could do about it, but he knew that if the gangster motioned toward his pocket, he was required to take a step forward. There was an understanding between everyone in the room that this was how it was supposed to be. The script had been written long ago and performed by other men in other rooms and in the movies.

Seeing this, the gangster grinned. He proceeded to feel around inside his jacket and then he extended his hand. In place of a gun was a business card.

"My gun, I keep down here," he said, raising the cuff of his left trouser leg. Strapped above his ankle was a pistol in a black, padded holster. "You see, we are civilized businessmen. Before we reach for that, we reach for this."

He placed the card on Skinny's desk.

"We manage very respectable artists. We provide security. Many good Russian restaurants in New Jersey and Brooklyn are our customers. There is a phone number on the card. It is our mobile phone. Think about what we said and call. If we don't hear from you, we'll come Saturday night to see for ourselves how successful you are."

After the gangsters left, Skinny Zyama picked up the business card and flicked it into his wastebasket. He passed his hand along the surface of his desk and examined his fingertips for dust. "Small-timers. Nobodies. Who do they think they're dealing with?"

Kostya waited for a few moments to see if he would say anything else. Zyama rapped his knuckles on the edge of the desk. He spun the knob of his Rolodex. He reached into a drawer for a pack of cigarettes.

"Is that it?" Kostya asked.

"That one sits staring like a mummy. The other one with the gun on his leg. Think they can intimidate me in my own place. I shit on them from a tall bridge," Zyama said.

That was Zyama's final word. He was Zyama Karp, no longer the grubby proprietor of the Pushkin Deli but the impresario of The Russian Riviera Restaurant. He was a man with influence. Not someone to be pushed around. And, after all, he also had Kostya, a Siberian boxing champion.

"If they come back on Saturday, you take care of them," Zyama said.

....

From The Russian Riviera, Kostya drove to the Prima Donna Ballet Academy to return a blouse that Ivetta had forgotten at his apartment. Ivetta frequently forgot things at his apartment only to discover that the thing she had forgotten was exactly the thing she could not live without. Kostya no longer resisted this; he had learned that it was best to simply return the item—a blouse, a pair of earrings, a lipstick—as soon as possible. He had also learned that once Ivetta resumed possession of these things, her need for them diminished.

Ivetta was waiting for him at the entrance to the ballet school. She took a moment to confirm that he had brought the blouse and lifted herself into the van.

"I have five minutes," she said. "We should drive around the block."

As Kostya eased the van onto the street, Ivetta turned to look up at her mother's office, on the second floor of the ballet academy.

"I think I see her standing there," Ivetta said.

Kostya interpreted this as a signal to drive faster, but when he accelerated Ivetta told him to slow down. If her mother was watching, Ivetta didn't want to give her the satisfaction of behaving furtively. Kostya didn't completely understand the rules that governed Ivetta's attitude toward her mother, but he knew that Luda Sorkina disapproved of him. Luda was a former ballerina. She was a cultured person. She was also a successful businesswoman. She had schooled her daughter in the fine arts, she had given her a university education, and she was grooming her to eventually take over the business. That such a woman would want more for her daughter than a failed boxer, a doorman and an illegal immigrant seemed to him perfectly reasonable. In fact, he could understand Luda's logic much better than Ivetta's. Why Ivetta should *not* want to be with him made much more sense than why she should. When Kostya had told her as much recently, she had led him from the bed to their reflection in his mirrored closet door.

"We are beautiful together," she said.

Kostya supposed they looked good. He still went to the gym five days a week and was conscious of his physique. And Ivetta had the long, slender muscles of a trained dancer. At the restaurant and on the street, Kostya was aware that men looked at her.

She was attractive in the usual ways, but Kostya's eyes were always drawn to the intricate places where different parts of her joined: her shoulders, her collarbone, the backs of her knees, her ankles, her hands.

"You could be beautiful together with someone else," Kostya told her.

"Then you don't see what I see," Ivetta said glumly, then moved away from him and hunched on the edge of the bed.

That he didn't see what Ivetta saw had been precisely the origin of the conversation, and so her answer did nothing to clarify things. Standing naked by the mirror, Ivetta's glum reflection over his shoulder, Kostya considered pointing this out but knew that if he did it would only further irritate her.

"You are honest and good," Ivetta had finally declared from her desolation at the edge of the bed.

And now, because he was honest and good, Ivetta wanted to protect him from Luda's sneering condescension. For this reason Ivetta had asked that he find someone else to work his shift on Saturday night, when her mother was going to make a rare appearance at The Russian Riviera.

"But I *am* a doorman," Kostya said. "What do I care how she looks at me?"

"I care," Ivetta said.

Most of her family would be there Saturday night, and she did not want to introduce him to them under those circumstances. If they were to meet him, then it would be done across a table, properly and with respect. Not with her family celebrating her grandfather's birthday while Kostya was relegated to the door or the bar: separate, an employee.

"Did you ask Ruslan?" Ivetta said.

"I will see him today at the gym."

Up until that afternoon, Kostya had been prepared to do just that, but now he couldn't imagine how it was possible. Ruslan was barely twenty and more eager to use his fists than his brains. Once or twice, when it had been absolutely unavoidable, Ruslan had substituted for Kostya at The Russian Riviera. On those occasions, Skinny Zyama had granted his permission, but he'd done so grudgingly. Zyama had expended considerable energy publicizing the fact that he had a Siberian boxing champion working his door—he'd oppose a change at the door even on a night without gangsters. And even if Zyama could be persuaded, Kostya's conscience would not allow it. Which meant that, as alternatives went, Kostya had two: he could work or he could quit. And, seeing as how he had no status, he preferred to risk the possibility of gangsters against the certainty of unemployment.

To Ivetta, of course, he could confess none of this. Her reaction would be predictable and extreme. She would go to Zyama or to the police. Both of which would mean the end of his job. Also, she would likely regard the situation as further evidence of their need to run off together and start a new life in another city, far away from her mother. She had urged him to do this before, to leave his demeaning job at The Russian Riviera, to escape somewhere, get married, go to school, start a business, buy a house, have children, live happily. The idea was tempting; Kostya had no attachment to the city or to The Russian Riviera, but, at thirty-four, he was also no longer a boy. If he quit his job, escaped with

Ivetta and she grew tired of him—a man without an education, with few talents, deficient in English—he was afraid that he would find himself back at zero. He would lose even the few things he had managed to accomplish.

....

At fourteen, in the gymnasium of the Number 4 High School, Kostya and his classmates, stripped to their underpants, had submitted to a series of physical tests administered by the head boxing trainer of the Omsk Spartak Athletics Club. The man had come and examined them; measured the lengths of their arms; with calipers, checked the thickness of the skin above their eyebrows; had them execute the standing broad jump and a complex version of hopscotch. Then, to eliminate criers and bleeders, he had punched each boy in the nose. From a class of twenty boys, he had selected three. Kostya had been one of them.

That day in the Number 4 High School gymnasium had altered the course of his life. Kostya could trace his few triumphs and his many hardships directly back to that day twenty years previous, and he often wondered what his life might have been like had his nose bled at the gymnasium, or had he quit the training sessions along with his classmates a month into the program. Possibly, he would have applied himself more at school. Maybe he would have entered a technical college and learned a trade. Tradesmen could always find work. He might have become a machinist or an electrician. But the problem was that in the gym, for the first time in his life, he had excelled. The mechanics and the theory of boxing had come naturally to him. There, unlike in the classroom, he hadn't needed to strain to understand. What's more, he had been encouraged.

This was in 1975, one year before the Olympics in Montreal. His trainer, widely known to be the son of an enemy of the people, had invited himself to Kostya's apartment to meet with his parents. In the communal kitchen, Kostya's mother served tea and condensed milk. The meeting was very formal, as though important business were being transacted. Kostya's trainer presented himself using his full name: Emil Osipovich Shtenberg.

"How would you like it," Emil asked, "if in five years your son was representing his country at the first Olympics to be held on Russian soil?"

"The boy's mother wants to know if he will be hurt," his father said.

"I would be a liar if I said he will not be hit, but you have my word he will not be hurt."

The discussion did not go much further.

"My wife and I have never been to Moscow," his father said.

"It is a marvellous city," Emil said. "I am sure you will enjoy it."

But though Kostya spent most of the next five years in the gym, his parents didn't get to go to Moscow. Since the Americans also didn't go to Moscow, Emil said it was just as well.

Any boxer who claimed to be Olympic champion without facing any Americans was a fraud. With this in mind, Emil fixed his sights on the future. For the Los Angeles Olympics, Kostya would be twenty-three, which in Emil's estimation was the ideal age for a middleweight. And so Kostya had persisted. Emil secured him a job at a furniture plant whose director, a boxing supporter, made generous allowances for Kostya's training schedule. Kostya received the privileges afforded to athletes: food coupons, a new track suit, occasional trips to cities in Western Siberia and northern Kazakhstan. Over time he also attained a degree of local recognition: girls smiled at him and men slapped him on the back.

By the winter of 1984, Kostya was middleweight champion of Omsk. Then of Western Siberia. To take the title, he beat a boy from Novosibirsk, opening a gash over his left eye and flooring him repeatedly with straight rights. After the referee stopped the fight, the boy sat on the canvas and wept. On the train back to Omsk, Emil admonished Kostya for showing too much sympathy.

"He can't go to his right," Kostya said, "and his mother has cancer of the pancreas."

"Whose mother doesn't have cancer of the pancreas?" Emil said.

"I don't see what's to celebrate."

"In life, any time you win, celebrate."

In this sense, Emil had been right. It turned out that fight represented the high point of Kostya's career. Soon after, he lost a split decision to a fighter from Chelyabinsk and once again failed to qualify for the national team. The fight had been close, but one of the judges had scored it overwhelmingly in his opponent's favour. When the announcement was made, the referee had had to restrain Emil from assaulting the judge.

According to Emil, politics had been at play. Kostya had been persecuted for the crimes of Emil's father. The authorities had not wanted to advance a fighter trained by the son of an enemy of the people. Fifty years earlier, before Emil was even born, Stalin had accused his father of Trotskyism, shipped him to Norilsk, and Emil had been paying the price for it ever since. Now Kostya was being punished as well. The system was vile and corrupt. Kostya deserved a spot on the national team, and it was only a small consolation when the Soviet Union boycotted the Los Angeles Olympics.

Under the strictest confidence, Emil told Kostya that he was finished with the Soviet Union.

"It so happens," Emil said, "my father was Jewish."

Laughing, he added: "Hard to believe that this would bring me anything except more grief."

A year later, Emil boarded a train and was gone. He promised Kostya a postcard from wherever it was that he landed. He promised to bring him over to the West, where his natural gifts would be rewarded. Kostya waited for the postcard but it never came. Gradually, he deviated from his training regimen. He spent more time with friends from the furniture plant, went to the *banya*, drank a little, got involved with women.

Occasionally, when he felt the urge in his back and shoulders, Kostya returned to the gym, but once there he felt like a guest. People recognized his face but fewer and fewer remembered his name. When he had been at the peak of his commitment, he had recalled seeing certain men come into the gym, men who had formerly been fighters, men who suited up and performed the old routines, but nobody took them seriously. For the most part, these men were easily distracted and did more talking than they did boxing. Even though he was still only in his twenties, Kostya saw that he had become one of those men.

In this way, like everyone else, Kostya lived his life. He watched the Seoul Olympics on television and felt only a passing sense of regret. When Russia began to change, he hesitated and did not join friends in business. He remained at the furniture plant until it was purchased by a consortium of Germans and Swedes. Afterwards, he took the kind of work available to him: physical labour, often outdoors. It was when he was working on a lumber crew, surrounded by men like himself—the anonymous many who were failing to prosper in the new Russia—that he received the letter from Emil. The envelope bore a Canadian stamp and a Toronto address. In it, Emil apologized for not having written in six years, but offered to make good on his promise to bring Kostya to the free world. The letter included specific instructions and a registered cheque for seven hundred American dollars.

....

Twelve years later than originally predicted, Kostya rode the train from Omsk to Moscow—only now his destination was not the Olympic Village but a travel agent's.

Partly because the Peruvians did not demand a visa, Kostya bought a plane ticket to Lima. Most of his money spent, he turned the remainder over to an old woman who claimed to be Emil's aunt. She provided him with a pillow and a wool blanket and helped him push a coffee table against the living room wall. Kostya stayed with her for three nights until his flight departed for Peru. On the plane he sat quietly, hoping in this way not to attract attention to himself. Most of the other passengers on the plane were Russians and Kostya wondered how many of them had the same intentions he did. It seemed strange to him that so many Russians would want to go to Peru. To him, almost all of them looked suspicious. He assumed that he looked suspicious as well and feared that one of the passengers or the stewardesses would denounce him to the pilot or some other authority. But when the plane set down for refuelling in Gander, Newfoundland, Kostya was invited to exit along with everyone else.

To his surprise, everything happened just as Emil had written. He followed the line of passengers down a long hallway and found himself inside the terminal. To prepare

himself, he chose a chair in the remotest part of the con-
course and went through the contents of his shoulder bag.
At the very bottom he found his sneakers. Doing his best to
casually conceal what he was doing, he peeled the insole off
his right shoe and palmed the scrap of paper he had hidden
there. Then he repacked his bag and walked the floor of
the terminal until he saw what he was looking for. Standing
near a newsstand was a woman in a uniform. Kostya did not
know what the uniform signified but it looked official. Willing himself forward, as though for an irreversible leap into
cold water, Kostya approached the woman and read from the
scrap of paper in his hand.

"Ya yem a refugee," Kostya said.

Subverting his every reasonable expectation, the woman
responded in heavily accented Russian.

"You want refugee status?"

"Yes," Kostya said.

"Follow me," she instructed.

Kostya spent two weeks in the refugee shelter in Gander
before he was claimed by Father Nikita, a Russian Orthodox
priest who operated a halfway house for Russian immigrants
in Toronto. When he arrived at the house, Emil was there to
greet him, talking immediately about his plans. That same
night Kostya moved into Emil's one-bedroom apartment in
the north end of the city. The apartment was in a building occupied mainly by Russians, flanked by other buildings
occupied by other Russians. Many of these Russians were

also Jews, though Kostya couldn't particularly tell the difference. On the main street there were Russian delicatessens, Russian bookshops, Russian video stores, and even signs and posters in Russian tacked onto the bus shelters and telephone poles. At the nearby park and at the playground, Kostya heard as much Russian as English. If he needed to go to the supermarket, there was always someone around to translate the labels. For Kostya, the non-Russian world existed only in the various gyms where Emil took him for their workouts. But even there, few demands were made on Kostya to communicate in any but the crudest ways. He learned the English vocabulary of boxing: jab, cross, hook, slip, uppercut. Also useful was the word *okay*.

....

Not long after Kostya settled in, Emil drove him to meet their benefactor. They made the short trip over in Emil's minivan, a van he had been using for years to deliver pizza.

"Don't talk unless you have to," Emil said. "And no matter what I say, don't contradict me."

The man they were to meet was Bomka Goldfarb. Before the collapse of the Soviet Union, Bomka had sold real estate in Toronto, but after the collapse he had returned to his native Kiev and made a fortune dealing in manganese. He was one of the richest Russian immigrants in Toronto.

Bomka set the meeting not at his offices but at a new Russian restaurant in which he held a partial interest. The restaurant was minutes away from Emil's apartment, situated in a strip mall. It featured, Emil had heard, a massive fountain in the foyer.

The fountain, Bomka Goldfarb explained when he greeted them, was a reproduction of one he had seen in Rome. When he had invested in the restaurant, it had been on the condition that it include such a fountain. The fountain was a marble sculpture. It reached almost to the ceiling and consisted of four fish supporting the torso of a powerfully built man. The man appeared to be either drinking from or blowing into a large shell. To Kostya's eyes, the man's face bore a resemblance to Bomka Goldfarb's.

Bomka directed them to a table near a broad stage that boasted a gleaming white piano. He bade them wait, then returned several moments later accompanied by a thin, pinch-faced man.

"This," Bomka said, "is my partner Zyama Karp. The restaurant is his vision." Bomka took a seat at the table, though Zyama remained standing.

"Zyama," Bomka said, "you should be acquainted with these people. Konstantin Petrov, boxing champion, and his trainer, senior Soviet coach, Emil Osipovich Shtenberg."

"A boxing champion?" Zyama asked.

"Very talented," Bomka said. "Emil came to me and said, 'How would you like to invest in a boxer?' I had been thinking about a racehorse. But Emil said, 'A boxer is cheaper and more interesting than a horse.' He'll be fighting at the Trump

Plaza, just as soon as we can get his immigration in order."

"Where were you a boxing champion?" Zyama asked.

"In Siberia," Emil said. "In 1984. He would have gone to Los Angeles if not for the boycott."

"Must have been very disappointing for you," Zyama said.

"You cannot imagine," Emil said.

"I was talking to him," Zyama said.

"It was disappointing for both of us," Emil said.

"What's wrong with him? Can't he speak?"

"Of course he can speak," Emil said.

"When do you become more interesting than a horse?" Zyama asked.

"What horse?" Kostya said.

"I like a sense of humour," Zyama said. "Did Bomka show you the dance floor?"

Zyama motioned for Kostya to rise and follow him toward the stage. Zyama indicated the floor.

"Stand here a moment," Zyama said.

Kostya stood on a transparent Plexiglas floor roughly twice the area of the stage.

Through the glass Kostya could see light fixtures, with multicoloured elements. As Kostya waited, Zyama mounted the stage and then stepped into the wings. He projected his voice from around a corner.

"Now watch," Zyama said.

Under Kostya's feet, the lights ignited and spun in their housings.

"Not even in Moscow or New York will you find something like this," Bomka said.

Kostya felt a mechanism engage with a hydraulic drone. Then, slowly, the floor began to elevate and a dense, white mist spread across its surface. The floor continued to rise until it came to a stop flush with the stage.

Zyama emerged from the wings, very satisfied, looking as though he had done more than spent money and pressed a button.

"Normally, I do not allow people to stand on the stage when it is activated. And only the performers of our Vegas-style show are permitted to use it. But I thought, for a boxing champion, I would make an exception."

The meeting ended with Bomka's renewed pledge to expedite Kostya's immigration process. In his employ, he had top lawyers. They were extremely well-connected. If asked, they could get asylum for Stalin.

On the drive back home, Emil was in very high spirits. More than once he volunteered that he was pleased with the results of their meeting.

"You made a good impression," Emil said.

"Why did you say I was a champion?"

"It's a word someone like Bomka Goldfarb understands."

"He'll be disappointed. I'm not the fighter I was six years ago," Kostya said.

"You're better than you think," Emil said. "Most American boxers aren't fit to tie your boots."

"But if you had written me six years ago," Kostya said.

"Six years ago I was delivering pizzas. And when I wasn't delivering pizzas, I was guarding the lobby of a condominium. So what was I supposed to write you? 'Dear Kostya, I have no money. The boxing establishment treats me like a nuisance. Nobody here cares if I live or die.' What would you have done with this kind of letter?"

Kostya thought that he would have liked such a letter. It wouldn't have changed anything but, thinking about the letter, he could see it on the tidy kitchen table, where his mother would have left it. He could see himself, in the evening, after the factory, sitting with the letter in his hands. He felt himself as though in that past. It was good to hear from Emil, to read about his troubles. It was good to think that, in a distant country, he had a friend who remembered him.

....

Ivetta never met Emil, but she had an opinion of him. She also had an opinion of Bomka Goldfarb and Skinny Zyama. It angered her that such people would deceive Kostya, and it angered her that he would allow himself to be deceived.

About Bomka and Skinny Zyama, there was nothing Kostya could say, but he felt obligated to defend Emil. Even if he had been deceived by Emil, it was only because Emil had himself been deceived.

"Bomka gave assurances and the lawyers gave assurances. Emil trusted them and I trusted Emil," Kostya said.

"Who in their right mind would trust a person like Bomka Goldfarb?"

"He paid Emil to bring me over. He sent a cheque each month for rent and expenses. We thought: Why would he do that if he wasn't serious?"

"Last month I bought a pair of shoes. Even at the store I wasn't sure I wanted them. But they were only sixty dollars. I wore them once. Long enough to become bored with them. Now they're in the back of my closet."

"It's true," Kostya said. "It's always good if you can afford to buy."

But if you couldn't afford to buy, things were different. And the nature of the difference could not be explained to someone like Ivetta, who had forgotten what it was like to be deprived. Ivetta would say that there are always choices, but after a certain point—even when looking back—Kostya could not see the choices. Would he have been better off in Siberia if he had declined Emil's offer? Should he have returned to Moscow with Emil? Could these be considered legitimate choices? To his way of thinking, confronted by the available options, he had always just pursued the least unpromising.

The same applied with respect to Bomka Goldfarb. Both he and Emil had been subject to Bomka's whims. Given the circumstances, what were their alternatives? Bomka had told them to sign papers, and so Kostya had signed papers. Bomka had told them to wait, and so they had waited. Occasionally, Emil made phone calls to ascertain the progress. He made the calls from behind his closed bedroom door, but the apartment was not large and the door was hardly soundproof. First, Emil had called the lawyers. Later, he had called an associate of Bomka Goldfarb's. Then, when the associate became unreachable, Emil left messages with a secretary.

To placate Kostya, Emil posed a rhetorical question: If Bomka has forgotten about us, why are we still getting monthly cheques?

The delay was understandable. Lawyers were notoriously slow. And who could compete with immigration officials—bureaucrats—when it came to laziness and inefficiency?

Emil counselled patience, but he paid a promoter to get Kostya on the undercard of a show in Windsor. This he considered money well spent—many of the fighters on the card would be Americans, and the whole thing would be broadcast on television in Windsor and Detroit. Also, the promoter had given his word that he would pit Kostya against a young fighter, a Golden Gloves champion, handled by smart people, expected to go far. But most importantly, the show would allow Bomka to see with his own eyes the value he was getting for his money.

The fight was scheduled for the February of a cold winter. To get to Bomka, Emil parked near his mansion and spent the pre-dawn hours wrapped in blankets, sitting in the van. Once Bomka left for work, Emil tailed him to his office. He waited an appropriate half-hour and then followed, bringing with him a box of chocolates for the secretary. When he recounted the story for Kostya, he stressed that Bomka had been very glad to see him—and particularly glad about the imminent boxing match in Windsor. So glad, in fact, that, to undertake the drive, he planned to hire one limousine for himself, his wife, kids and Skinny Zyama, and a second limousine solely for Emil and Kostya.

"I hope you refused the limousine," Kostya said.

"You don't want the limousine?"

"Someone who hasn't won a fight in six years shouldn't arrive in a limousine."

"To be honest," Emil said, "I don't entirely disagree, but this isn't something I could have explained to Bomka Goldfarb. Here's what I suggest: if it bothers you, ignore it's a limousine. Pretend it's the van."

But the limousine, a black stretch Cadillac, was not easy to ignore. As soon as they climbed inside, the driver drew their attention to the bar, the television, the VCR, the selection of Russian videos, and the refrigerator stocked with smoked meats and caviar. Everything compliments of Bomka Goldfarb.

"He has a fight today. No food. No alcohol. No distractions," Emil said.

"Too bad," the driver said.

"That's the way it is," Emil said.

"It's four hours to Windsor," the driver said. "A long time to stare out the window at nothing."

"Elite athletes must be focused," Emil said.

"No doubt," the driver said. "I was never an elite athlete myself, but I know something about it. My daughter is a dancer and my ex-wife was a prima ballerina. Danced with Baryshnikov."

"Very interesting," Emil said.

"Boxer," the driver said. "If you get bored staring out the window, say the word, I'll tell you my life story."

Eventually, Kostya heard his story, though not before he and Emil arrived at the Bavaria Club in Windsor—a low two-storey building with a wooden roof and white stucco walls. From the parking lot and the entrance, it resembled either a restaurant or a modest hotel. Obeying signs and arrows, Emil and Kostya located the Sports Hall; there they discovered a ring encircled by several rows of metal folding chairs and a handful of people—easily identified as other fighters and trainers waiting for the weigh-in. Emil had never met the promoter in person and so was forced to approach a number of them before being directed to a man younger and fatter than Bomka Goldfarb. The man saw Emil coming and, despite the look on Emil's face, extended his hand and smiled. Emil leaned into the promoter's face, ignoring his outstretched hand, and started shouting—mainly in English but partly in Russian. Kostya understood only the Russian, a collection of obscenities bred of the prison camps and the army.

After Emil finished his tirade, he stalked back to Kostya.

"We could call Bomka," Kostya said. "Say the fight is cancelled."

"No use," Emil said. "We're fucked."

In a limousine, somewhere between Toronto and Windsor, Bomka, his wife, his two sons and Skinny Zyama were eating and drinking the things Kostya and Emil had denied themselves. Kostya could picture them all, including Bomka's wife and children, even though he had never laid eyes on them. He imagined them in the Sports Hall, dressed for the casino but installed on the metal folding chairs, in a half-empty room decorated with German banners and dingy photographs of the German countryside.

"What do you want to do?" Kostya asked.

"We came here to fight; we fight," Emil said.

Fourth on the undercard, Kostya fought. His opponent—no young Golden Gloves champion—was a grim, heavily muscled black fighter who, in place of satin trunks and boxing boots, wore army surplus shorts and basketball shoes. Outside the ring, with a weapon, he would have been the sort of man Kostya would have been happy to avoid, but inside the ring, restricted to using only his hands, he was plodding and mechanical. Had he cared about the promoter or the spectators, Kostya might have tried to carry the fight into the second round. But there was nobody to impress. Bomka's wife had taken one step inside the Sports Hall, paused, spoken three words and then she, Bomka and the children had disappeared. Only Skinny Zyama remained, and so he was able to watch Kostya joylessly punish the black fighter to the body and then stop him with a left hook to the temple.

Afterwards, by way of congratulations, Skinny Zyama handed Kostya a Russian Riviera matchbook.

"Call if you want a job," he said.

....

In the summer of 1974, Mikhail Baryshnikov defected in Toronto. In 1978, at the Jewish Joint Distribution Committee office in Rome, Luda Sorkina brandished the letter Baryshnikov had written to her. The letter was not long, but in it, Baryshnikov devoted an entire paragraph to Toronto. A little provincial perhaps, Baryshnikov mused, but a good place to start a ballet school.

"At the Riga Ballet, I danced with Baryshnikov," Luda Sorkina informed the case worker.

Luda Sorkina displayed this same letter when the family met with a diplomat at the Canadian embassy on Via Zara; she showed it to her remedial English instructor at George Brown College—having had it translated shortly after the family arrived in Toronto; and when she applied for a small business loan from the Jewish Immigrant Aid Services, she carried the letter, her diploma and a Latvian newspaper clipping that included a photograph of herself dancing with Baryshnikov.

Seated at the bar of The Russian Riviera, Volodya Sorkin told Kostya, "There wasn't enough room in the marriage for the three of us."

"You, her and Baryshnikov," Kostya guessed.

"Me, her and the letter," Volodya said.

Volodya was a regular at The Russian Riviera. He came not as a diner, but as a patron of the bar. On nights when his limousine wasn't booked, when he used the car for fares to the airport, Volodya stopped in to catch Ivetta's performance in the Vegas-style floor show. Before the show, he nursed a drink and talked to whomever was around—mostly to Kostya, who had little to do but sit at the bar. Fights and confrontations were uncommon. The clientele at The Russian Riviera was predominantly middle-aged, educated and relatively well off. Also, it was Jewish. In this respect, Kostya discerned a cultural difference between Russians and Jews: on the rare occasion when there was trouble, nobody pulled a knife.

Through Volodya, Kostya became acquainted with Ivetta. Kostya hadn't had much interaction with the dancers and musicians, who socialized mainly with one another, but he had taken notice of Ivetta. Not because of some striking physical attribute—with the costumes and the makeup, all of the dancers looked like slight variations of the same woman—but because she possessed a quality Kostya had observed in the best athletes: she gave the impression of effortlessness. It was the illusion that the forces of time and gravity did not apply equally to all people.

Her face and neck still flushed with the charge of the performance, Ivetta slid in beside her father at the bar. She kissed Volodya affectionately, and seemed to take no note of Kostya until Volodya turned inclusively in his direction.

"This is my good friend Kostya," Volodya said.

"Very nice to meet you, Kostya," Ivetta said.

"Kostya is a boxer," Volodya said.

"Was a boxer," Kostya said.

"Not anymore?" Ivetta asked.

"I wouldn't say so."

"When were you a boxer?" Ivetta asked.

"It depends who you ask," Kostya said.

"I asked you."

"Then I would say six years ago."

"And if I asked someone else?"

"Then they might say two weeks ago."

Ivetta fell silent, arched her head and studied him. She seemed to be contemplating something, but Kostya couldn't imagine what. The expression on her face made Kostya wonder if she had misheard what he had said. It was possible, maybe because of the noise in the restaurant, that she had heard not the words he said but instead some strange words that sounded like them. Kostya thought to repeat himself but reconsidered. Instead he told her that he had seen her dance.

"She's the star," Volodya said.

"She's very good."

"Nice of you to say," Ivetta said.

"If I could move like you, I would still be boxing."

....

On subsequent nights, even when Volodya wasn't there, Ivetta took to joining Kostya at the bar. At first, she did so seemingly without intention. After the show, she would pass by the bar, evidently on her way somewhere else, and discover Kostya— unexpectedly, as if for the first time. Kostya would see her brushing past and invite her to sit. Later, the pretense was dropped.

Initially, their conversations centred on Kostya's boxing and his life in Siberia. Ivetta seemed interested in things that Kostya found mundane if not embarrassing. But since she claimed a genuine interest, Kostya told her the details of the furniture plant, his boxing trials with Emil, his empty years after the fall of Communism.

Ivetta spoke about her life with her mother and her own ambitions. Ivetta had been nine when her family came to Toronto and sixteen when her parents had divorced. Her father had worked for years as a taxi driver to support them while her mother tried to establish her ballet school, but once the school was established, she discarded him. In Riga, Volodya had been a civil engineer, but in Toronto he could not find a job in line with his qualifications. Later, when her mother asked for the divorce, she said it was because Volodya was no longer the man she married. She had married an intellectual, an engineer; now she lived with a cab driver.

To Kostya and Ivetta, independently, Volodya said, "I hope you know what you're doing."

Passing them at the bar, Skinny Zyama said, "Don't get her pregnant. It will kill my show."

The night Ivetta finally went home with Kostya, they left the restaurant in separate cars. Kostya drove ahead in Emil's van and Ivetta followed in a new Nissan Maxima. At the parking lot, Kostya felt the urge to apologize for his car, and in the apartment, he felt the urge to apologize again. Clearly, she was used to better. All he could offer was what Emil had left him. He hadn't changed anything in the apartment since Emil had departed, cursing the apartment and his possessions—everything he had acquired in his time in Canada. He had never belonged here, he'd told Kostya, and he'd felt, every day, an exile. A man in his fifties should not come to a strange land, not knowing the language, absent connections, and expect to thrive. He had abandoned his homeland because of a pernicious system, but now that the system had been overthrown, he would return. He would go to Moscow, where he could restore his reputation. The borders were open. Russia was replete with talent. A Russian fighter could now ply his trade all over the world—in Europe, in America, in Australia.

"Keep everything, including the van," Emil had said. "The ministry mails the registration renewal in October. They have it organized by birth month. Mail them a cheque and send me a birthday card."

Kostya slept on the same mattress that Emil had salvaged years before from Goodwill. His furniture consisted of a metal and Formica kitchen table with mismatching pine chairs; a faded grey velour couch; a coffee table with a scored glass top; and a large Zenith television set in a wooden console.

But in spite of the shabbiness of the apartment and the van, Ivetta didn't complain. Even as she spent increasingly more time there, she never once suggested that Kostya replace the table or the bed. Thursday, Friday, Saturday and Sunday nights, after The Russian Riviera, they drove to the apartment in their separate cars. On the other nights, Ivetta slept at her mother's house. Finally, when Luda Sorkina confronted her, Ivetta fled to Kostya's apartment in tears. She threw herself onto his bed and bawled. She stayed like that for a long time, her back shuddering—either imploring or forbidding Kostya to comfort her. When Kostya laid his hand on her, Ivetta related the painful details of her argument with Luda. Her mother had said cruel, shameless things. Ivetta increased her sobbing when she told him the worst of them.

"At least your father was something before he became nothing," Luda had said, "but you, you're starting with nothing."

....

On Saturday, at eight o'clock, in among the arriving guests, Kostya spotted the face of the larger gangster and then that of his smaller companion. Kostya watched them drift from the door to the fountain. The larger one settled in to Kostya's right and his friend took the next seat over. After nodding to Kostya, the larger gangster asked the bartender for two cognacs, and, when each snifter had been filled, he made no move to pay.

"We're guests of Zyama Karp's," he said. The bartender glanced at Kostya.

"It's fine," Kostya said.

"Where is your boss?" the gangster asked.

"Around," Kostya said.

"Tell him we're here."

Kostya rose from his seat and walked the length of the bar to Skinny Zyama's office. As he passed the gangsters, he remarked that they were both dressed the same as before— with the curious exception that the smaller gangster had holes in his socks. He was seated on his bar stool with his legs bent, and the holes exposed white, hairless skin.

Kostya found Zyama standing before a full-length mirror, adjusting his suspenders and straightening his bow tie. His shoes were poised beside his desk and his tuxedo jacket was draped over the back of his captain's chair.

Turning from the mirror, Zyama eyed Kostya.

"Fix your tie," Zyama said.

Kostya fingered the knot of his tie and gave it a superficial tug.

"The gangsters are here," he said.

"What gangsters?"

"The New Jersey gangsters."

"What are they doing?"

"Drinking at the bar."

"Sons of bitches."

"What do you want me to do?"

"Get rid of them," Zyama said. "Just don't make a scene."

On his way back, Kostya paused to transfer a set of brass knuckles from his breast and into his left trouser pocket. Typically, he did not carry a weapon. Any problem he could not solve with his fists was likely a problem he could not solve. But in this instance, anticipating the gangsters, he had brought the brass knuckles as a limited precaution. He felt their weight against his thigh and checked to be sure that their outline was not visible through the fabric.

At the bar, the larger gangster was smoking another cigarette and surveying the foyer and the dining room. He watched Kostya's approach.

"You told him?" he asked.

"You should finish your drinks and leave," Kostya said.

"Is that what he said?"

"No. He just said leave."

"He's making a big mistake."

"Someone is," Kostya said.

"Maybe even you." The gangster smiled.

The gangster remained on his stool. Whatever would happen would not happen just yet, Kostya sensed. The initial crush of guests were then assembling in the foyer—a collection of witnesses and complications.

Kostya left the bar and took up his position by the door, where he oversaw the familiar procession. Moguls in designer suits—their fortunes amassed in the wake of the Soviet collapse—parked their Bentleys, BMWs and Mercedes and ascended the steps accompanied by their bejewelled wives. Lesser businessmen and professionals—there to celebrate birthdays and significant anniversaries—trooped from Hondas and Toyotas carrying flower arrangements, cake boxes and bottles of vodka. Amid the disorder of coats and the near-suffocating fog of rival perfumes and colognes, Kostya saw Ivetta and her mother approaching—both looking elegant and unhappy. As they neared Kostya, they became more unhappy. With them were an old man and an old woman—Ivetta's grandparents. Her grandfather was clean-shaven, his hair full and white. He wore a brown suit and, for his age, moved precisely and energetically. Her grandmother, unlike most women her age, had hair that was neither dyed nor cut. Instead, her grey hair was gathered in a bun. She wore a colourful shawl over an oriental-looking dress and held her husband's arm. When Luda addressed Kostya, the woman abided patiently.

"So you're him?" Luda said.

Before he could answer, Luda turned to Ivetta.

"Is this him?"

"Yes."

"Where are your manners? Why don't you introduce us?"

Painfully, Ivetta made the introductions.

"Mother, Kostya. Kostya, my mother."

"Why so formal?" Luda asked. "We may be in-laws. We should embrace."

That said, neither she nor Kostya inclined to embrace.

"Who is he?" Ivetta's grandfather asked.

"Ivetta's boyfriend," Luda told him.

"We invited him?" the grandfather asked.

"He works here."

"Is that so?"

"He's the doorman," Luda said.

"The doorman?"

"Yes."

"Does it pay well?" the grandfather asked.

"All right," Kostya said.

"Cash?"

"Yes."

"By the hour?"

"A flat sum for the night."

"What about tips?" the grandfather asked.

"Not usually."

"You live in a house or an apartment?"

"An apartment."

"Where?"

"Antibes."

"We used to live there. How many bedrooms?"

"One."

"What do you pay in rent?"

"Seven hundred dollars," Kostya said.

"Expensive. You should save up, get a house."

As her family proceeded into the dining room, Ivetta

lagged behind, her face dark with hostility. Keeping a sterile distance from him, she said, "How could you do this to me?"

She spoke loudly enough to cause people nearby to turn their heads. In private, Kostya thought he might have been able to contend with Ivetta's anger, but in public he felt inhibited by shame. The feeling was the same he had experienced as a boy, singled out before the class, shifting by his desk, the radiators ticking.

"I only asked for one thing," Ivetta said.

"If it was possible, I would have done it," Kostya said.

"Do you care about me at all?"

"Yes," Kostya said.

"No. If you cared about me, you would have never let this happen."

With a cool finality, Ivetta pivoted on her heel and stranded Kostya in the foyer. He watched as she struck across the floor and into the dining room to join her family. For the first time, he felt the desire to hurt her. He had never done it before, never hit Ivetta or anyone, man or woman, in anger, but at that instant, there was a pressure in his hands and his shoulder blades that wanted release. If he had been asked to describe the pressure, he would have said it amounted to the phrase, repeated: Who needs this? If he was able to step outside or find a quiet corner, Kostya thought he could contain the feeling. If he could blind himself to Ivetta in the dining room, to the people jostling him, to the gangsters at the bar, he could arrive at a solution.

Only a few steps and he could be outside, where he could breathe and think. But as he pressed toward the door, he saw the larger gangster waving to him, a leer in his square face, and Kostya did not resist.

"That's some girl," the gangster said.

Without answering, Kostya resumed his seat at the bar.

"A good figure and a temper. The sort that likes it rough. Gets down like a dog; begs to be slapped around."

The guests were all in the dining room now, sitting down to their excess of food. Soon the band would start up. Lyona Ostricker would assume the stage and sing Russian classics and then coarsen his voice and do an imitation of a famous black jazz singer. Guests would toast the objects of their celebrations. Bow-tied waiters would deliver the first course. The dance floor would fill and the band would play Russian and American disco.

"This isn't going to end well," Kostya said.

"For who?" the gangster asked.

"Good question."

"It doesn't have to be this way," the gangster said.

"It does if you stay," Kostya said.

At the far end of the dining room, near the stage, Skinny Zyama was holding court at his usual table. Guests and acquaintances stopped by to pay their respects. The choreographer, a woman twenty years his junior, kept him company.

"You don't expect us to leave without seeing the famous show?" the gangster said.

"The show is an hour away," Kostya said.

"We came this far, we'll wait," the gangster said.

Kostya regarded the smaller gangster. He sat coiled and seething, his eyes feverish. For the duration of the hour, until the show began, he held the same position. But when the lights dimmed, the people cleared the dance floor, and the prelude for the spectacle began, he started to shift in his chair. And when the dancers—Ivetta included—assumed the stage for the *Fiddler on the Roof* number, the smaller gangster lowered himself from his seat and made for the men's room. Without a word, the larger gangster followed.

The Vegas-style floor show normally lasted half an hour. What intermittent changes the choreographer imposed never altered the length of the show. The guests came with the expectation of a half-hour's entertainment by versatile performers. After the *Fiddler on the Roof*, there was something in which the dancers leapt across the stage dressed like cats; then there was a scene from *Swan Lake*; then a song called "Cabaret," for which Ivetta was the lead. Kostya had seen this incarnation of the show at least thirty times and had memorized its rhythms to the extent that he could hear the words and visualize the steps before they were executed. And he knew that after the end of *Fiddler on the Roof*, there remained more than twenty minutes in the show—twenty minutes during which the guests' attention would be concentrated on the stage.

Quietly, suppressing the impulse to hurry, Kostya crossed the length of the foyer to the men's room. On the way he placed his left hand in his pocket and slipped his fingers into the brass knuckles. With his right hand he pushed open the heavy men's room door. To the right were eight tall porcelain urinals. To the left was a long expanse of black marble floor, and six white marble basins on nickel pedestals. The walls were covered with gilt-framed mirrors, and by the door were two brass tubs—one filled with fresh linen towels, and the other with a pile of the same towels, already soiled. Opposite the basins were four ceiling-high toilet stalls—slabs of black marble with nickel-plated doors. The washroom was spotless and silent. Kostya listened for some indication of the gangsters. Down the line, using his knee, Kostya tested the stall doors. The first two swung open but the third held fast. At the disturbance, a voice belonging to the larger gangster said, "Occupied." Kostya jostled the door again.

"Fuck off," the gangster said.

Gauging his distance, Kostya reared back and slammed his heel against the door. The bolt gave way, and the door flung inwards to reveal the two gangsters. The smaller one was seated on the toilet, and the larger gangster squatted in front of him. It took Kostya a moment to decipher what they were doing. The smaller gangster had his jacket off and one of his shirtsleeves rolled up. A belt was cinched at his biceps and a syringe protruded from his forearm. So far as Kostya could tell, the man did not look conscious.

From his position on the floor, the larger gangster gave Kostya a look of animal hatred.

"My brother is sick," he said.

An instant later he sprang up. Kostya moved reflexively, slipped to his left, shifted his weight and threw an uppercut that caught the gangster's jaw. He felt the force of the blow through the brass knuckles and into his shoulder. He could not remember when he had hit anyone as hard, and he felt a shiver of pleasure descend through his knees. The gangster tottered to one side, bumped against the stall and then pitched backwards onto the floor. He lay there, prostrate, breathing raspingly. Kostya saw blood on his face and shirt collar and a spreading pool, oily black, on the dark surface of the marble.

For a time the only sound in the room was breathing. Kostya heard his own, that of the beaten gangster, and the slow, nasal exhalations of the smaller gangster, slumped against the toilet tank. Kostya tried to settle his pulse and clear his mind. Both men were breathing; they would live. Kostya had contained the mess to the washroom, and if he acted quickly he could summon Skinny Zyama, remove the gangsters and clean up without disturbing the guests. Nobody could accuse him of failing to do his job, but Kostya derived little contentment from this. The job was something he no longer wanted. The thought of pleasing Skinny Zyama or of sitting at the bar another night to watch Ivetta dance seemed unendurable. It occurred to Kostya that he could leave the gangsters to be discovered by Skinny Zyama or someone else. He could walk away. While the show was still on, he could leave without attracting attention. He could find another apartment and another job no worse than this one. It did not need to be difficult.

Kostya took another moment to compose himself. He examined his hands and saw blood. If he stepped out, he could not step out covered in blood. But before he could consult the mirror, he heard movement at the men's room door. Kostya blocked it with his foot.

"Busy cleaning. Use the women's room," he said.

"The hell I will," the man replied and kept pushing.

Kostya slipped his fingers back into the brass knuckles before he released the door and Ivetta's grandfather forced his way in.

"There's been an accident," Kostya said.

"I can see that," Ivetta's grandfather said.

The old man bent and examined the gangster's broken face.

"It only looks bad," Kostya said.

"I was at the front. I've seen bad."

He walked over to the smaller gangster and placed a hand on his chest.

"Still beating," the grandfather said.

The old man then stepped into the neighbouring stall and urinated. When he finished he moistened a towel in the sink and handed it to Kostya.

"There's blood on your face," the old man said.

"It's his," Kostya said.

"He needs an ambulance," the old man said.

"If you think so," Kostya said.

The music for "Cabaret" flowed into the washroom as the old man opened and closed the door. As the door swung shut, Kostya's thoughts turned to his own grandfather. The man had died when Kostya was still young, but Kostya could recall sitting with him as he related stories of the Great Patriotic War. A German grenade had taken three fingers off his left hand. On the back of the hand, he had the date and place of the battle tattooed in green ink. At that time, reminders of the war were everywhere. There were tributes and parades to honour the veterans. Movie theatres showed documentaries and heroic epics. In the streets and back lots, Kostya pretended with his friends that they were the Red Army on the attack. To cries of "Forward, comrades!" they rose from culverts and trenches and charged across the steppe, rifles pointed, greatcoats flapping. Kostya hadn't thought about any of this in years, though at one time he had dreamed of glory on the battlefield. Later, these dreams were supplanted by dreams of the ring.

Kostya failed to notice that the smaller gangster had begun to stir until the man half-raised himself from the toilet. Kostya watched with a measure of sympathetic curiosity as the gangster scanned the room, absorbing the details: the broken door, the blood, his brother's disfigured face. He lifted his eyes to Kostya as if seeing him for the first time.

"Where am I?" the gangster asked.

"The Russian Riviera," Kostya said.

The gangster rocked on his feet and spread his arms across the stall, his elbows locked, his torso tilted forward.

Kostya expected him to collapse at any moment. He looked like a fighter who had gotten up when he should have stayed down, whose pride and courage would only be rewarded with a harsher beating.

"How did I get here?" the gangster asked.

"I don't know," Kostya said.

"How do I get out of here?"

"I don't know that either."